CW01065302

"I would not be here had it not been for poor Bob."

Lieutenant Peter Clivedon's voice betrayed his emotions.

"If the notion is not repugnant to you, Miss Hammond, I would like to do what I can to fill the gap he left," he said.

Helena struggled with grief and confusion. "I am sorry, Mr. Clivedon. I do not seem to understand."

He stood before her with an odd, scared look in his shadowed grey eyes. "Miss Hammond, I ask the honour of your hand in marriage!" he explained.

"Good heavens!" gasped Helena. "But you scarcely know me. Or I you."

"I know that you are good, and kind, and—er, gentle." Peter flushed, and stammered on. "I am a wealthy man. I can offer you a good enough house in town, and I've a very nice place in Sussex at your disposal."

"I see," said Helena, looking quickly away. He did not really want this, poor fellow, but clearly he felt duty-bound to provide for the lady of the man who had given his life to save him.

Peter's voice interrupted her thoughts. "Miss Hammond, have I your permission to speak to your Mama?"

In that instant, Helena's mind was decided. She smiled at him gratefully.

"I cannot refuse your kind and noble offer, Mr. Clivedon. You have my permission."

Further Titles by Patricia Veryan from Severn House

POOR SPLENDID WINGS
LOVE'S LADY LOST

MEN WERE DECEIVERS EVER

Patricia Veryan

This title first published in Great Britain 1993 by
SEVERN HOUSE PUBLISHERS LTD of
9–15 High Street, Sutton, Surrey SM1 1DF.
First published in hardcover format in the USA 1993 by
SEVERN HOUSE PUBLISHERS INC of
475 Fifth Avenue, New York, NY 10017,
by arrangement with Harlequin Enterprises B.V.

British Library Cataloguing in Publication Data
Veryan, Patricia
  Men Were Deceivers Ever
  I. Title
  823.914 [F]

  ISBN 0-7278-4541-1

Typeset by Hewer Text Composition Services, Edinburgh.
Printed and bound in Great Britain by
Redwood Books Trowbridge, Wiltshire.

Sigh no more, ladies, sigh no more
Men were deceivers ever;
One foot in sea, and one on shore;
To one thing constant never.

—William Shakespeare
Much Ado About Nothing

CHAPTER ONE

December, 1811

LONDON WORE HER WINTER DRESS, and on this frigid afternoon that dress was of grey, relieved only by the occasional white flutter of a snowflake carried on the chill wind. Christmas was less than a week away, and the many shoppers walked quickly, noses buried in their scarves as they clutched their treasures, eager to get home before the light failed altogether.

From an upper window of a small house off Fitzroy Square, a young lady pressed her cheek against the cold glass, peering eagerly towards the corner around which the long-awaited caller must come. Her big brown eyes brightened as a chaise turned that blustery corner, then slowed. The girl held her breath as she waited with eager anticipation for a glimpse of military scarlet, and a dark curly head.

The postboys shivered as they guided the team along the quiet little street. In the chaise, Lieutenant Peter Cliveden listened with only half an ear to the endless chatter of his youthful charge. Peering into the dusk, he lifted one gloved hand at length, and inserted in his quiet way, "Hold up for a second, halfling. Is this your house?"

Master Emmett Hammond paused in his elaborate description of his adventurous journey from Harrow, took up his shallow crowned hat, and turned his bright dark eyes from his companion. "Lord, no, sir," he laughed. "That's the Chalfont house. They're full of lettuce—not like us! There's my house. That little red brick one squashed between the two grey giants."

Cliveden lowered the window, admitting an icy blast, and shouted to the postboys. The chaise came to a halt, the horses breathing clouds of steam to mingle with the misty air. The lieutenant let down the steps. "Don't forget your parcels," he adjured with a grin. "Here, I'll take the valise."

Engulfed by the boy's gratitude, he ushered him across the flagway, up the six steps, and rang the bell. It was a rather cosy little house, he thought, the candlelight turning the frost-edged windowpanes into squares of gold. The door swung open. Accompanied by a delicious smell of cooking, three cats raced out, one startling Cliveden by leaping onto the valise he carried, and then shooting after its companions. "Jove," he gasped.

The dark young gallant who stood in the opening, laughed and ruffled Emmett's similarly dark curls. "Rascal! Mama and your sister have been beside themselves!" His gaze turned to the tall army officer. "I suppose you rescued him, did you sir? Blasted little pest! Come in, come in. Never stand there freezing." Raising his voice, he yelled, "He's home, everyone!"

Miss Helena Hammond already knew that her errant youngest brother had returned. Her heart had leapt when the young officer stepped from the chaise, only to sink again when the candlelight from the downstairs windows had played upon light brown hair having a slight crisp wave, rather than revealing glossy black curls. But her disappointment had been banished by delight when Emmett had sprung from the vehicle. She was already running to her mother's room, calling, "Mama! He has come! Emmett is safe!"

Cliveden heard that musical feminine voice as he handed the valise to the man on the step. "I must be on my way. I've a postchaise waiting, and—"

"Pay the boys off! No, I will! You must allow us all to thank you. Dine with us—unless you're under orders, of course?"

"No, but—"

"Oh, do stay, sir!" Emmett tugged at his arm. "You must! Rostyn, make him! It smells as if we're to have steak and kidney pie for dinner, and—"

"Kayne," howled his brother. "Give me a hand here, you lazy lout!"

There came the sound of quick light feet. This, thought Cliveden, stunned, could not be "Kayne" for any fellow describing this heavenly vision as a "lazy lout" must be demented.

"I'm Rostyn Hammond," the dark man explained, clapping him heartily on the back even as he pulled him into the fragrant hall. "Oh, that's my sister, Helena, and this great lout is my brother. Come on Kayne! We've to bring in this fellow's belongings."

"No, but—but really," stammered Cliveden, staring at the slender girl who was exchanging an enthu-

siastic embrace with Master Emmett. He was jolted by
another clap on the back from a sturdy young giant
who strode past, smiling at him and saying in a deep
amiable voice, "Hold this, will you?"

An enormous ginger Persian cat was thrust into
Cliveden's unready arms. Kayne Hammond paused,
and said over his shoulder, "That's First Cat, by the
way. Hello, Mama," he added, raising his eyes to the
stairs.

A tiny little woman hurried across the hall, her
pretty face beaming with joy. She was pale and fair,
her high-piled hair streaked with silver. Very neatly
dressed in a blue velvet gown, she flew to embrace
Master Emmett, pausing only to thrust a large black
cat at Cliveden. He took the new addition under his
left arm, and continued to stare at the girl.

During his brief twelve years, the escapades of the
irrepressible Master Emmett Hammond had several
times brought his female relatives to the brink of nervous collapse, and his mother and sister had become
somewhat hardened to his close brushes with an early
demise. They had not really worried when the boy was
two hours late in returning from a short visit with a
schoolmate prior to spending the Christmas holidays
at home. When five hours had crawled past the
expected time of his return, however, Mrs. Hammond had been on the verge of sending out her elder
sons in search of him. Now, helping him out of his
heavy coat, Helena smiled in silence at Emmett's
bright young face, since she was quite unable to break
into his excited monologue.

"... And the stagecoach overturned just outside some miserable village called—What was it, sir?" asked Emmett, blithely disregarding his mother's and sister's cries of horror.

"Wembley," supplied Cliveden, balancing cats. She must be about eighteen or twenty, he thought, approximately five feet two inches in height, and with the kindest smile and the prettiest little mouth he'd ever seen. She had the same colouring as her brothers, but there the resemblance ended. She was delicately formed, her shapely figure complemented by the pink velvet tunic over the white silken gown. Her luxuriant dark brown hair was worn high, the curls charmingly threaded by a pink velvet ribbon. Fascinated, he watched her, and she watched the boy patiently as he prattled on.

"Yes, Wembley. Only I wasn't hurt, just thrown onto the fat lady's basket of eggs and wasn't she cross! Luckily none of the horses was badly injured. All because a foxed dandy wanted to tool the coach! Some gentlemen drove up and took passengers who were travelling in their direction, only most of them were going north you know, and then this very obliging officer came and volunteered to bring me home, which was jolly nice because he's just back from Spain on leave, and—"

Without warning the black cat and the large Persian First Cat took one another in dislike, and reacted with fang, claw, and loud feline obscenities.

Well scratched, Cliveden hurriedly released them both.

"Good gracious!" For the first time Miss Hammond gave her full attention to the tall soldier. 'Past twenty-five, but under thirty,' she decided. He snatched off his cockaded hat, and the thick light brown hair tumbled attractively over his brow. She took quick inventory of a rather thin face with a humorous mouth and strong chin, and thought his best feature was a pair of thickly lashed grey eyes that held a shy smile. "How rude we are," she said, liking him at once.

"Yes indeed," agreed her mother. "Pray present your rescuer, Emmett."

"Jove, but I'm sorry sir," said the boy. "Lieutenant Peter Cliveden, this is my mama, Mrs. George Hammond, and my sister Miss Helena Hammond."

Wrenching his attention from the sparkling dark eyes and enchanting dimple, Cliveden bowed. The ladies curtseyed, and Mrs. Hammond said, "How very grateful I am, sir. We must talk later, but First Cat caught you properly, I see. Take him into the kitchen and wash that scratch, Helena. And you shall certainly stay for dinner, Mr. Cliveden, unless you've some pressing former engagement?"

"What're you about now, Mama?" called Rostyn, carrying Cliveden's valise in and bringing a bluster of cold air with him. "Poor fellow, do they not allow you to go past the front hall before they are telling our family secrets? Besides, your betrothal ain't official yet, Helena."

She was betrothed, thought Cliveden. Logical enough.

Helena said pertly, "Mama referred to a dinner engagement, brother dear. Come, Mr. Cliveden. Take his coat, Rostyn."

Handing over gloves, hat and coat, Cliveden thought, 'No butler? No manservants at all?' and decided they must be properly in the basket. Yet the house was comfortably, if not luxuriously furnished; all the male Hammonds were clad in the latest fashion; and the ladies' gowns bore the unmistakable mark of a skilled modiste. Besides which, Harrow was an expensive school. 'A pity,' he thought, 'if they're living on tick only to keep up appearances.'

Helena showed the lieutenant into the kitchen. Running what he mistakenly imagined to be a tidying hand through his hair, he reiterated, "I really must be on my way, ma'am. I merely gave your brother a ride, and there is no call for you to feel—"

"Obliged?" She regarded him with a smile that awoke little lights in her big dark eyes. "Oh, but of course we are! And now I must present you to our incomparable housekeeper. Verny, we have a dinner guest. Mr. Cliveden has brought dear Master Emmett safely home to us. Mrs. Vernon, sir."

A very fat woman turned from the stove, bobbed a curtsey and said earnestly that she was sure they all were most grateful to the gentleman. She had a round face that fairly glowed with cleanliness, and the apron about her broad middle was like snow. She did not appear to find it odd that a stranger should be brought into her kitchen, and she sent her two buxom maids scurrying into the dining room to put out another cover.

The lieutenant was required to sit down at the immaculate table. Mrs. Vernon came bustling over with a bowl of warm water, some strips of linen, and a jar of salve, and Helena proceeded to bathe the scratches. "We were really becoming quite worried about Emmett," she said. "He is the youngest and Mama's darling, as you may guess."

"He's a fine fellow. Bright as a guinea, but not at all spoiled."

Busied with linen and salve, she smiled and said, "And chattered your head off all the way here. There, I think that will help matters, and I hope you will forgive us for treating you so shabbily after you were so kind as to rescue my brother. I suppose he has told you all about us."

"Only that your Mama was widowed four years ago, and that Rostyn is a great gun but rather hot at hand, and Kayne has a punishing right—which I can well believe. May I ask if your Papa was a—" he blinked as one of the maids returned, two white cats trailing after her, "—a military man, Miss Hammond?"

Helena led him towards the door again, picking up one of the white cats en route. "No, sir. Papa was extreme opposed to warfare." She glanced at him curiously, thinking that he looked rather tired. "Perhaps you have heard of another Hammond who is in the army?"

"No. It is just that not everyone is aware that a lieutenant is addressed as 'mister.'"

"Oh, I see. Well, I must tell you that—" she looked down, a faint blush warming her delicate features,

"—that one of our closest friends is a Captain. Indeed, if Rostyn had his way—"

"He'd be in Spain with Lord Wellington," put in her oldest brother, coming into the hallway. "Hurry up, Nell. We want to talk with our guest, you can't keep him all to yourself, you know."

There was much talk when they adjourned to the cozy withdrawing room. Lieutenant Cliveden was ushered to the deep chair closest to the fire, and had no sooner sat down and been given a glass of wine, than Mrs. Hammond launched into heartfelt expressions of gratitude and praise for his efforts in behalf of her "lost one." His protestations that he had done very little, since he was driving this way at all events, were brushed aside. She'd already had it from Emmett that Mr. Cliveden was on his way to Sussex. "In which case," she said, smiling mistily at him, "I expect you would have avoided the metropolis and gone straight into the country, had it not been for your kindness in restoring a stranded boy to his mother's loving arms." She continued in this vein, painting such a glowing portrait of Cliveden's unselfish gallantry that he was heartily grateful when Rostyn laughingly told his mama to stop embarrassing their guest into an early grave.

"Hear you've just come from Spain, Cliveden," he went on. "Seen any action?"

"A little."

Kayne asked eagerly, "What is your regiment, sir?"

"The Fifty-Second, of course," said Emmett scornfully. "Do you not see the buff facings and silver lace?"

"Revolting little pipsqueak," said Rostyn without heat.

Kayne inserted knowledgeably, "Then you were at Albuera."

There was much exclamation at this, and Emmett gave a squeak of excitement. "*Never* say so! Do you know Colonel Colborne? Is it truth that his Light Brigade was wiped out by Polish lancers?"

Cliveden's grey eyes darkened. After a brief pause he said in a low voice, "There was a beastly hailstorm, and we were blinded. The lancers were all over us before we knew it."

"Was you sent home because of wounds?" asked Rostyn.

"What's his lordship really like?" put in Emmett eagerly.

Kayne leaned forward in his chair. "When do you go back?"

With a slow smile Cliveden looked from one bright face to the next.

Helena laughed in a musical little trill that he thought delightful. "Good gracious, you tyrants! Give the poor gentleman some peace!"

Before Cliveden had a chance to do more than glance at her amused face, his peace was quite destroyed. A pretty golden-coloured cat which had been eyeing him speculatively from the right side of the chair decided to take possession of his lap at the same instant that a grey cat on the left side of his chair formed the same resolve. They both leapt, collided in mid-air, and cats and Madeira were scattered in all directions.

Through the ensuing uproar, Helena at last heard the sound for which her ears had been straining and her heart leapt. A moment later the door swung open and a deep voice filled with laughter cried, "Good Gad! What a commotion!"

Wiping Madeira from his hand, Cliveden came to his feet with the other men and turned to meet the newcomer.

A tall young Captain strolled into the room. Beautifully built, and darkly handsome, he would have commanded attention in civilian clothing. In the full splendour of his uniform, his curly head held high and proud, he was magnificent. He crossed at once to bow to Mrs. Hammond. Then he was standing before Helena. She knew she was blushing, and looking up into his ardent eyes, her own were like stars. "Good evening, Lord Robert," she said in her soft lilting voice. "You are come just in time for dinner."

He bowed over her hand, his thanks drowned as Kayne strolled over to clap him on the back, and say with a grin, "D'you think he didn't know that?"

"Oh, now you must not tease him," scolded Mrs. Hammond fondly. "My lord, we've a new friend with us. May I make you known to Lieutenant—"

"Peter Cliveden!" The newcomer turned with a warm smile to the Lieutenant. "Jove, but I had thought you was downed at Albuera!"

Shaking hands, Cliveden said quietly, "I got up again, as you see, Bob."

"Well, I'm dashed glad of it. Leave, old boy? Or despatches?"

Aware that every eye was on him, except for the loveliest pair which were fixed on Captain Lord Robert Eastleigh, Cliveden murmured, "Both, actually."

The dinner gong was rung. To Cliveden went the honour of leading his hostess into the cosy, wainscoted dining room. Branches of holly adorned the mantel, a fire burned on the hearth, and five cats of various shapes and sizes were crowded before the blazing logs. The table was set with creamy napery, and candles sparkled on crystal and silver and revealed another adornment which caused Cliveden's eyes to widen.

Rostyn said an irked, "Oh, egad! Get the brute off!"

Helena ran to remove a large black cat who'd been napping on what turned out to be Cliveden's plate. To his relief she also removed the plate and rang for the maid to fetch a clean one.

As soon as grace was said, Cliveden was bombarded with questions about the campaign in general, and the Battle of Albuera in particular. He replied politely, but was not sorry when Eastleigh said, "Let the poor fellow be, you fiends. He don't want to talk about all that."

"Why not?" demanded Emmett, who, having reached the age of twelve, was allowed to dine with the adults. "It was his lordship's most glorious victory, no?"

"Glorious indeed," said Rostyn enviously. "What I'd give to have been there!"

Cliveden frowned. "You would have had a glimpse of hell," he said. "Your pardon ladies, but there is no other word. It was ghastly."

There was a small, pregnant silence.

Eastleigh laughed suddenly. "Just like old Peter. In on the battle of the century, and don't see anything of the glory, only the gloom!"

"I saw fifty of our finest leaders wiped out in the wink of an eye when we scaled the wall," said Cliveden, his fingers tightening around the stem of his glass and his face suddenly without colour. "Before we'd finished it I had lost every one of my closest friends. To say that our casualties were appalling would be an understatement. If that is your idea of 'glory,' Bob— it's not mine."

The other men exchanged uneasy glances.

With an edge to his voice, Eastleigh said, "Then you should better have been a Hyde Park soldier, old boy!"

Cliveden had been raising his wineglass. Briefly, his hand paused, then continued. He said nothing, but met the other man's eyes steadily.

"Well, here we are," boomed Kayne. "Almost done with 1811, and jolly good, say I! What with the Society for the Suppression of Vice, and—"

"Yes, only think, the self-righteous dimwits managed to put an end to Sunday rowing matches and boat races on the Thames," chimed in Rostyn indignantly. "Dashed unfair!"

"It does seem rather harsh," Helena murmured. "Especially for the poor, who have only one day a week in which to seek amusement."

"You know, my dears," said Mrs. Hammond, removing the tabby who was climbing up one end of the tablecloth, "Hannah More says that the amusements of a Christian must have nothing in them to excite the passions."

"Excite the passions, indeed!" exclaimed Rostyn. "If ever I heard such stuff about rowing a boat!"

They all laughed, and the ensuing chatter was kept carefully innocuous. When the two ladies left the gentlemen to their port and cigars, Helena was sure her mother would refer to that sudden moment of tension. Mrs. Hammond's somewhat erratic mind had been elsewhere, however, and her remarks were all of either her dear Emmett or the peerless Lieutenant Cliveden.

The gentlemen joined them quite soon, and Helena was asked to play her newest piece, a sonata by Mr. Handel. Cliveden's attempt to listen to the melody was foiled when Mrs. Hammond passed him a tortoise-shell cat as one might confer a great favour, and then engaged him in a steady flow of low-voiced conversation. His was a sympathetic ear, and in no time his suspicions were confirmed. He learned much of the late Mr. George Hammond's disastrous losses on 'Change, and of the endless pennypinching required of the widow so as to keep "dearest Emmett" at Harrow.

Before the tea tray was carried in, Cliveden murmured to Rostyn that he really must be on his way. A whispered counter-offer of a comfortable bed was regretfully declined. The rain had stopped and a full moon was bathing the city with light; Cliveden was anxious to reach his country estate before morning. Rostyn said he would send their groom to the livery stable to hire a postchaise, and the two men slipped unobtrusively from the warm, pleasant room.

Engrossed in her rendition of a traditional air, and happily conscious of the adoration in a pair of fine green eyes, Helena scarcely noticed them leave; a fact of which Lieutenant Peter Cliveden was very aware.

"YOU'RE NOT COLD?" Captain Lord Eastleigh drew Miss Hammond's hand through his arm and started off along the now deserted flagway.

A sudden gust of wind whipped the hood of her pelisse from her curls, but she scarcely felt the chill of the night air, happiness bathing her in a warm glow that no exterior force could dim.

Restoring her hood, Eastleigh gazed down at her dainty features, and said softly, "I vow, Miss Nell, you are lovelier each time I see you."

"Fie upon you, Sir Flattery," she teased. "And with Mrs. Cutterleigh watching us from her parlour window, too!"

He chuckled and glancing to the imposing mansion beside them, said, "Gad, but you're right. We'd better step along, ma'am, for I've to report back to Whitehall by eleven."

The smile faded from her eyes as they walked on. "You're not going to leave us, my lord? I had thought you were to stay in Town for some time."

"So had I, ma'am. But I'll not deny I'm eager to go. Wellington needs trained officers."

The hand on his arm shook. She gasped, "Are you for Spain, then?"

He checked and smiled down at her. "Why the worry, sweet lady? Is it because of what Cliveden bleated? Never heed the fellow. He's a dull dog."

"But he has been in the fighting. He knows—"

"He knows how to pour cold water onto things. Always has. Even at school. We went to a cock-fight once, and saw a most excellent bout; both birds were game as a pebble and fought to the death, and all Cliveden could say was it was 'needless cruelty!' Pshaw! You'd never believe his father is a General! On the Viceroy's staff in India now, I think."

She said hesitantly, "He spoke with such anger. It must have been a dreadful battle."

"Oh, some fellows simply cannot face action. I'd not have taken Peter for a coward, but—" He caught himself up. "The army's a dashed fine life, Nell. I've been trying to interest Rostyn and Kayne in joining up."

"Pray do not! Rostyn is wild to go, but—we have lost Papa, and Mama would be heartbroken was anything to—"

"Never fear," he interrupted soothingly. "They say they've not the funds to buy their colours. But if every man stayed home for the sake of his Mama, old England would be in sorry case, I fear."

"Yes." She hung her head. "I know it is wrong to be so spineless. Are you to sail very soon?"

They had come to the small garden in the middle of the square. Unlocking the gate with her key, Eastleigh ushered Helena inside, and leading her to a seat, replied, "And if I was, would that sadden you, lovely one?"

"You—know it would," she faltered shyly, uneasily conscious that it was exceedingly improper to be alone with him in this moonlit privacy.

He pulled her to him. "How sad?" he asked, his voice husky. "Sad enough that I might suppose you to have an affection for a simple soldier?"

"You are not a simple soldier! You are from a distinguished house and Viscount Burtonbrook's heir besides."

"And you are the loveliest, the most adorable, most kissable lady in all old London Town!"

Helena's heart seemed to melt before the ardour in his eyes. She offered no resistance when he took her in his strong arms and tilted her face up gently. His kiss was long and hard, and she was trembling and breathless when at last he released her lips. "Oh... Robert...." she whispered.

"Have I your leave, my dearest," he murmured, "to ask your mama's permission to pay my addresses?"

It was the answer to her dreams. She had to fight very hard to be sensible. "But there is our disastrous financial situation to be considered. Papa lost near everything on 'Change. Mama has only a small competence, sufficient to keep the house and servants and one carriage, but she has to struggle to pay Emmett's fees at Harrow. And—"

"If I am accepted my dearest girl, I shall have the right to pay Emmett's fees."

She shook her head dubiously. "And your great-uncle? What will Lord Burtonbrook think of your offering for a penniless girl?"

He laughed, and pressed a kiss into the palm of her gloved hand. "He will be *aux anges*. He is very proud, you know, and your lineage is such as must please the old duffer." He tilted up her chin, and smiling into her shining eyes, demanded, "Well, ma'am? Dare I hope it would not disgust you to be named Lady Robert Eastleigh?"

Yielding to the pressure of his arms, disgust was the farthest thing from Helena's mind.

CHAPTER TWO

CURZON STREET WAS THRONGED with carriages, and the great house of Viscount Ajax Burtonbrook was ablaze with light. Flambeaux on either side of the wide front doors illuminated the steps and the flagway, and lamps and candles brightened every window. On this unusually mild March evening the sounds of music and laughter drifted forth to entertain the crowd gathered on the flagway to ogle the clothes and jewels of the mighty. The reception hall was a crush of guests curious to meet the well-born but impoverished girl who would wed Robert Eastleigh. Standing between Lord Burtonbrook and Mr. William Eastleigh, Helena was a picture in an off-white satin ball dress, the train hand-embroidered with large feathers in varying shades of green, while smaller but similar feathers adorned the low-cut bodice. Her dark hair was swept into thick coils high on her head, with tendrils curling down beside her small ears. The only jewellery she affected was a dainty pearl pendant which had come to her through her maternal grandmother; and her betrothal gift—a diamond bracelet.

Her hand ached, and she was beginning to tire. She had lost count of the number of guests she had welcomed, comparatively few of whom were known to her since the viscount's secretary had made up the invitation lists. Most of those attending were familiar by repute, if not by acquaintance. The cream of the Top Ten Thousand, thought Helena, uncomfortably aware that these haughty ladies and flirtatious gentlemen had come not to pay homage to her or Robert, but to please the formidable gentleman at her side. Her bright smile gave no hint of her unease, nor of the fact that she was not very happy. This evening, which should been have such a triumph, was shadowed by the absence of her beloved, for Captain Lord Eastleigh had sailed for Spain in February, taking with him her two dear brothers.

When arrangements had been made for the Ball which was to introduce Miss Hammond to the ton, it had been thought that the prospective groom would be home on leave. The leave had been cancelled, however, Lord Wellington having remarked that in his "humble opinion" England would be better served by the presence of Captain Lord Eastleigh at the head of his men in Spain, than at the head of a reception line in London. Viscount Burtonbrook was irritated, but, refusing to postpone the ball, had forged ahead with the preparations, apparently clinging to the belief that his nephew would return in time to attend.

Mr. William Eastleigh, a shy youth who had come down from Oxford to act for his brother at the ball, moaned softly into Helena's ear, "Gad, does this go on forever?"

She smiled at him, glad that he could feel sufficiently at home with her to make such a remark. At one and twenty, William was thin and gangly, having his brother's colouring, but few of his good looks. He was a kind boy, however, and Helena liked him very much and was most grateful that he had not abandoned her to stand here alone beside his awesome great-uncle. Before she could respond, the stout, red-faced Marquis of Stover was making his bow. He ran an appraising and impertinent glance over her, gripped her aching hand with thoughtless violence, roared something incomprehensible about a "demned fine-looking gel," then said quite audibly, "Brought the boy to heel Ajax, begad but y'did!"

Helena heard a muffled snort from William. The odd remark must have been, she decided, in regard to his attendance tonight, for she was quite sure he did not willingly stand in his brother's shoes. Seconds later the enormous case clock in the corner tolled the hour of midnight, and Lord Burtonbrook decreed that they had done their duty. Turning his cold pale eyes on his grand-nephew, he added, "It is time for Miss Hammond to be seen on the dance floor. You may lead your future sister into the ballroom now, Eastleigh."

"Thank you, sir." With an ironic grin, William offered Helena his arm.

The viscount, tall, well built and haughtily elegant, put up his quizzing glasses and devastated the boy with a stern stare. Then, at his stateliest, he wandered off to be at once surrounded by his cronies, the set of wealthy gentlemen who wielded such power in Society.

"Phew," sighed William. "Those old fudsoys will keep Boringbrook in the card room 'til he's too foxed to know where he is, thank God!"

Helena gave a gasp. "You wickedness! What if he heard you? Does Lord Robert know you speak of the viscount in so disrespectful a way?"

He looked at her anxiously, saw the twinkle in her dark eyes, and chuckled. "Bob started it, so do not blame me. I say, Helena, do you really want to dance? I'd trample all over your dainty slippers, and—"

"Nell!"

A short, rather insipid looking fair girl wearing a pale blue gown that added to her washed-out appearance, was hurrying across the hall, arms outstretched. Helena gave a cry of delight. "Geraldine! Oh, I am so *glad* you could come!"

The two girls, who had for three years attended the same young ladies' seminary, embraced happily, and Mr. Eastleigh made good his escape.

Miss Geraldine Savage was full of apologies and regrets for her late arrival. "I had *so* wanted to come early, for we have so much to chat about, but my brother takes longer at his toilette than do I!" Her blue eyes surveyed her friend mournfully. "And now I fancy your dance card is full, so we'll not be able to have a single moment together."

"Indeed we shall," said Helena. "My poor feet are on fire, and I can think of nothing I'd rather do than to have a cose with you while I rest them for a little while." With a cautious glance in the direction of the card room she whisked Miss Savage along a side hall and into the most secluded of the ante rooms. With a sigh of relief Helena sank onto a glorious gold brocade sofa and drew her friend down beside her. "Now, dearest, tell me what you have been about. I've not seen you for—an age!''

"What *I've* been about!'' Miss Savage's chuckle brought dimples into her plump cheeks. "You're the one has caught yourself a peer, you saucy rascal! I've never so much as seen your affianced. Is he—'' She interrupted herself to ask with fond concern, "What is wrong, Nell? Never say this is a *mariage de convenance*, and Lord Eastleigh old and evil, and repulsive to you?''

Helena gave a peal of laughter. "My fiancé is the dearest, most handsome, most brave gentleman I ever met.''

"Aha! You're in love with the lucky man. Then why so sad?''

Dismayed, Helena said, "No, do I seem unhappy? How very bad of me.''

"No one would suspect it, save those who know you well. And if I am trampling where I should not tiptoe, you may forget I spoke. I am tactless as ever, alas. Small wonder I'm an old maid, and likely ever shall be.''

"Old maid, indeed! What rubbish. You are—what is it?—nine months my senior? An ancient twenty-year-old! And with that fair hair and your blue eyes—''

"And the fact that I am too fat,'' inserted Geraldine with a sigh.

"Pleasingly plump, rather. Which many gentlemen consider an attribute rather than a failing, dear.''

Miss Savage smiled, her eyes veiled suddenly. "Some do, perhaps. But when am I to meet your beloved?"

"Not tonight, alas. He is gone to fight with Lord Wellington. And," Helena added ruefully, "I must be a very weak woman, because it is wrong to worry. They are brave men, fighting for the land they love, and without them heaven knows what would become of us. But sometimes I grow so fearful. The battle for Ciudad Rodrigo sounds to have been even worse than Albuera, and so very many killed! I cannot deny that I *do* worry. And I so miss them all."

The faint colour in Miss Savage's cheeks vanished. "Them... all?"

Helena nodded. "Lord Eastleigh holds the military to be a good life for a young man, and my brothers needed little convincing. They applied to my Uncle, Sir Tobias Neilsen, and he was pleased to purchase their colours. I had feared Mama would be prostrated, but she is proud rather, and boasts to all her acquaintances of her two soldier sons."

"Do you say that Rostyn and Kayne both wanted to go to Spain? One cannot but—but honour their gallantry."

Geraldine's voice was rather unsteady, and Helena scanned her curiously. "Yes, indeed. Bless them, they were wild to go and help fight that Corsican monster. And Rostyn said it would help Mama because he and Kayne would no longer be eating up all our food." Her smile went a little awry. "I only wish I had just a little of their courage, and could—"

"So here you are! Well, at least we've arrived in time to go down to supper, sister mine, and—" The raspingly bored voice checked, and the broad-shouldered gentleman who had sauntered to join them checked also, raising a jewelled quizzing glass to one heavy-lidded blue eye. "Here we have a pretty creature," he drawled, inspecting Helena with impudent admiration.

He was in the neighbourhood of thirty, not above average height, but most elegant in his evening dress, and was blessed with curling brown hair and regular, well-cut features. Helena thought him very unlike his sister, for while Geraldine's blue eyes were full of fun and kindness, his were hard and cold, and his lips were thin, with a cynical twist she could not quite like.

Miss Savage shook her head at him. "Do not be at your flirting, rascal. Come and let me reacquaint you with my dear friend Miss Helena Hammond. My brother Leopold, Nell. I believe you met once when we was at school."

"I recollect only a spotty girl with pigtails," he said outrageously, bowing to touch his lips to Helena's fingers. "Not a delectable goddess. Allow me to take you in to supper, lovely one. I must eat before I face the hapless sacrificial bride, else I shall be quite unable to sustain it."

"Sacrificial!" Half-annoyed, half-amused, Helena extricated her hand. "You've an odd way with words, Mr. Savage."

"Leo," moaned Geraldine, scarlet with embarrassment, "*do* pray stop being so naughty! Miss Hammond *is* the sac—prospective bride!"

Staring, he exclaimed, "*You*? But I was of the impression—" He stopped, then made a fast recover. "Eastleigh is to be congratulated. Really, Miss G. If you'd seen fit to inform me of the name of the promised lady—"

"I *did* tell you. Several times. But you were busy nursing your grievances because you were obliged to escort me here, and paid me no heed."

"How was I to know such delights awaited?" His smile unexpectedly charming, he offered Helena his arm. "Shall we fly from this nest of asinine aristocrats? I've a fast coach and four."

"This is my betrothal ball," she reminded him, trying not to smile.

"Yes, but I heard you say Eastleigh had persuaded your brothers to join up. You certainly won't want to wed him after such villainous conduct."

The smile died from Helena's eyes. "Sir, I honour our fighting men, and am proud my brothers serve with Lord Wellington."

"Oh, egad," he groaned, clapping a hand to his brow. "Blinded by the glorious uniforms, are you? What a very great pity you ladies are so gullible. I suppose were I to buy a pair of colours you might regard me more kindly! No, do not refine on it. I've no inclination to suicide, even for so lovely a creature."

"Leo!" cried Miss Savage. "You go too far!"

He chuckled. "Then perhaps I *shall* consider suicide."

Helena said coolly, "I fear I have been too long away, and Lord Burtonbrook will be justly vexed do I not appear at my own ball." Ignoring Leopold's sardonic sneer, she smiled at the distressed Geraldine. "We must talk again, dearest, but for the present I beg that you will excuse me."

Geraldine waited in silence until Helena was out of sight, then turned on her brother with an anger she rarely showed him. "You are a horrid person, Leo! I've not seen Miss Hammond for an age. *Had* you to spoil it for me?"

"I rather fancy the lady has—er, 'spoiled it' for herself. But I'll not reproach you for your cruel insults. I'm glad you dragged me here."

"Something set you off." She scowled at him, then asked shrewdly, "What were you about to say when you realized Helena was betrothed to Eastleigh?"

He shrugged and stifled a yawn. "I cannot recall."

"Yes you can. You said you was under the impression—and there you stopped. Why?"

"Hmm..."

"What is that to mean? Oh, come along, Leo. You seldom curb that acid tongue of yours. What is it you are reluctant to tell me?"

Despite a rather unsavoury reputation, Leopold Savage was genuinely fond of his only sister, and now he eyed her with faint amusement. "I may have an acid tongue, my good girl, but I do not gossip about my friends."

"Goodness me, how excessive proper you are become. And for how long has Robert Eastleigh been a friend of yours?"

He tapped the quizzing glass against his chin, murmuring an infuriating, "I wonder.... It quite eludes me."

"I'm not surprised," Geraldine said dryly, then added in a cajoling way, "But, you do know him, Leo?"

"Oh yes." He glanced at the open door through which Helena had gone. "I know Captain Lord Robert Eastleigh. I wonder if Miss Hammond does."

"YOU DO NOT KNOW your affianced very well, dearest," pointed out Mrs. Hammond, trying gently to remove the brush from the jaws of Jasmine, the tortoiseshell cat, so that she might groom First Cat, who occupied her lap. "When *did* we meet him exactly? I cannot seem to recall."

Deftly sewing flowers into the poke of the primrose yellow bonnet she would wear to church on Easter Sunday, Helena smiled at the thought of her beloved, and said, "Why we have known him forever, Mama. We first met I suppose, when we would drive to Harrow to visit Rostyn."

"Mmm," said Mrs. Hammond. "Now Delilah, be good! Oh dear—now she has your thread, Helena! Rostyn thought Eastleigh very great, I recall. I wonder why your Papa never liked him. But we did not really *know* him, did we? Not until Rostyn chanced to meet him at Drury Lane in the Spring."

At considerable risk Helena retrieved the yellow thread from the beautifully marked brown-and-white cat named Delilah, and said, "You see, you do remember, dear."

"Yes, but you have spent very little time in Lord Robert's company, after all. Oh, you danced with him several times at parties. No, you must not eat the brush First Cat, and pray allow me your tail. And he has taken you up in his carriage on a few occasions. But how well do you really *know* him, dear?".

Helena blinked. "I know I care for him, Mama. And I know he loves me, else he would never have offered for a portionless girl." And beginning to suspect the cause for this gentle interrogation, she asked, "Are we *really* in the basket, dearest? We seem to go along well enough."

"Certainly we do. You must not think me a widgeon, Helena, for—Do not *bite* Soot! There are so many ways to acquire funds that it quite surprises me to recall how very depressed dear Papa became when his investments failed."

A chill crept down Helena's spine, and her busy needle was stilled. "To...acquire funds, Mama?" she echoed. "However does one go about that?"

The little woman smiled at her fondly. "Well, you must not tell Rostyn, my love, for he became quite huffy when he found out I had borrowed a few hundred guineas—a trifle really—from dear Uncle Tobias."

Helena paled, and put aside her almost completed bonnet. "But, Mama, Uncle Tobias was so good as to purchase my brothers their colours, and—"

"Good gracious, don't be such a ninny, child! Certainly I shall not ask him again. But you'd not believe how many other kind gentlemen are willing to help. There is a Mr. King, for instance, who has the nicest house on Leadenhall Street, and is so obliging. And I must not forget Mr. Brinkman who lives in a very strange sort of place near the Embankment." Her brows knit and she said with faint censure, "Rather depressing. But a most *understanding* person, although one cannot quite like the way he bows all the time. And then there are the two gentlemen named Mr. Levy and—"

Helena pressed a hand to her throat and said in the thread of a voice, "Do you say that these men are all *moneylenders*? Surely, you—could not—"

"Oh, but I could," declared Mrs. Hammond, triumphant. "Which just goes to show, my love, that gentlemen do not know everything! Why, when I merely mentioned the matter to Kayne before my darling sons sailed away, he laughed and told me I should catch cold at that." She giggled and said confidingly, "A naughty little bit of cant dearest, which means I should never be able to do it. They would not lend to *us*, says Kayne, for everyone knows we are only half a leap ahead of the constable. I was quite taken in, and for a long while made no attempt to try and bring us about. But then, well, I simply did not have the funds for Emmett's school fees this year. And the bank has been so patient, Helena, and let me pay as I could, but at last writ me such a polite letter, saying I really must make good on the arrears—"

"Arrears...!" whispered the stricken Helena.

"Yes. Though I do not recall buying any of those, I must admit. And then Mr. Murchison came to see me—such a dear man—and pointed out that the loan I'd taken out on the house—*Helena!* Pickle is sleeping in your new bonnet!"

"How...nice..." gulped Helena, numbly, wondering what the boys would do when they came home and found they had to go to Newgate to visit their family. "So that is when you applied to the—er, 'gentlemen'?"

Mrs. Hammond smiled at her fondly. "You was always quick witted, dear child. I did not dare use our own carriage, for it might be recognized, you know. Besides," she lowered her voice and said in a stage whisper, "it does not do to let the servants know one is short of funds, else they start to ask for their back pay! So I hired a hackney cab, and the—jarvey, I think he is called, took me about so nicely. I was just a teensy bit nervous, you know. Because of what Kayne had said. But he was as wrong as he could be. Oh, I'll own they were a trifle disagreeable at first, but they soon realized I was one of the Quality, and I had no trouble at all."

"But—what did you put up...as collateral?" managed Helena, feeling decidedly faint.

"Ah!" beamed Mrs. Hammond. "So you *do* know that word! I told Mr. Brinkman you would! 'La, sir,' says I, 'I've no least notion what you mean by that! I should have fetched my daughter with me, for she is clever—for all she's pretty as any picture, and is in fact betrothed to Lord Eastleigh.' And do you know, dearest, Mr. Brinkman became all that is conciliating, and gave me *twice* what I had asked for! Wasn't that *kind* of him! And it was just the same with the other gentlemen."

'Oh, mercy!' thought Helena dazedly. 'She has borrowed against my marriage!' "Whatever," she whispered, scarcely aware she spoke audibly, "would Lord Burtonbrook say?"

"Yes, I had thought of going to him first," confided her mother, sublimely disregarding her daughter's horrified yelp. "But he seems rather starched-up,
do you not think, love? And I would do nothing to
spoil your prospects. Not for the world." She smiled
at Helena lovingly, then frowned a little, and went on,
"Only the hackney man said something about my
payments! It seems they cannot wait until a person is
in funds again, but expect one to pay them—in *advance*, as it were, which I think stupid, for how can
one make payments if one has not yet found any more
money? Pray do not look so troubled, my sweet. You
yourself told me that Lord Robert had promised to
pay dear Emmett's expenses. And I have no doubt
Lord Burtonbrook will make us a most generous settlement when you are wed, so that we may give the
nice gentlemen their money, and they may be comfortable again. But I *did* receive rather a funny letter
from Mr. Levy yesterday, so I wanted just to be sure,
you see my love. Lord Robert *will* hold true to his
promise... won't he?"

Helena had seldom been more frightened. Poor
Mama. She had no least notion of what she'd done,
but it was very obvious that they were in deep debt,
and from what Kayne had once said of moneylenders, there would be the most ghastly interest piling up
every day! She thought frantically, 'Oh, if only Robert were here! If only my dear brothers were home!
Something must be done, and quickly. But—what?
She caught herself up. Mama was looking at her with
dawning anxiety in her sweet little face. She must not
be upset, or they would likely have her suffer another

of those terrifying attacks that had plagued her when poor Papa went to his reward.

She drew a deep breath. She could do nothing on Good Friday or on Saturday, and not for the world would she spoil Emmett's happiness during his short holiday. They would all go to church on Easter Sunday, and have a jolly day together, and next week she would find someone to advise her. "Of course Lord Robert will keep his promise, dearest," she said staunchly. "He is the very soul of generosity. Never fear, if worse comes to worst, I can write and ask him to help us. Now you must get out of my bonnet, Pickle." She dispossessed the white Pickle and foiled Soot's dastardly attempt to take his turn at occupying the rather crushed straw. Shaking out the bonnet and coaxing it back into shape, Helena put it on and turned a smiling if pale countenance to her mother. "How shall I do on Sunday, dearest?"

Mrs. Hammond beamed at the beautiful face so softly framed by the primrose lace frills and the silk pastel flowers. "Oh, my love," she sighed happily. "How *very* pretty you are! All the ladies will loathe you!"

She was probably correct, for on Sunday morning Helena won many admiring glances. The new bonnet was a perfect complement to the primrose gown she had fashioned with her skilful hands and which cast into the shade many gowns other ladies had purchased at great expense from London's leading modistes. The India muslin was trimmed by a deep flounce overlaid with fine white lace. The short bodice also was overlaid with lace. She wore a simple strand of pearls, and white elbow-length gloves, and carried the white reticule Mrs. Vernon had made.

Many a male eye wandered admiringly in her direction, and among these was a bored blue pair which brightened as they discovered her. Coming out into the rather breezy sunlight, Helena drew her shawl higher about her shoulders, and was startled when a gloved hand rendered assistance.

"Good morning, Miss Hammond," drawled Leopold Savage, bowing. "Only see whom I have found, Geraldine. Your school friend."

Miss Savage left the vicar, and greeted Helena happily. While the two girls chattered, Leopold, nobody's fool, devoted his attention to Emmett and Mrs. Hammond. The end of it was that he insisted they all must be his guests for luncheon. Helena was dubious, but Emmett was overjoyed, and Mr. Savage appeared to be on his very best behaviour. His luxurious barouche conveyed the ladies to Vauxhall Gardens, Savage and Emmett following in the Hammond's shabby old landaulet. After a delicious luncheon, they boarded a boat and were rowed along the busy River Thames for an hour. The afternoon sun had become warmer, and the whole city seemed to have turned out in its Easter finery. Master Emmett was in high fettle, and Helena was gratified to see her mother's pretty face bright with happiness. All in all, they had a very nice day, and Helena could not but warm to the gentleman who had so annoyed her upon their first meeting. Not until they were returning to Vauxhall did Savage show his true colours.

"What have you heard of your noble suitor, Miss Hammond?" he enquired blandly. "A letter every day, I'll warrant."

Helena flinched inwardly. She had received not one letter from Lord Robert, a fact which caused her much heartache. "A soldier has little time to write letters, Mr. Savage," she replied loyally.

"Really?" He smiled his cynical smile. "I'd have supposed a man in love would find time to write even as he marched. But never despond. If Eastleigh neglects you, I'll be only too willing to take his place."

Mrs. Hammond laughed merrily. "Such a naughty brother you have, Miss Geraldine! What a good thing we know he does not mean what he says."

Savage gave his sneering laugh, Geraldine hurriedly changed the subject, and her graceless brother behaved himself for the rest of their time together.

Lying in bed that night, Helena knew that her first impression of Mr. Savage had been the right one, and she wondered how so sweet a girl as Gerry could have such a nasty cynic for a brother. She could still see the mocking smile in his cold blue eyes. How dared he suppose she would ever glance his way? Sooner would she wed the dustman! Or that quiet soldier who had brought Emmett home last Christmas, and spoken in such a cowardly way of the Battle of Albuera. But she was safely betrothed to the man of her dreams, and there was absolutely no reason to be troubled by the memory of a sardonic voice saying, "A man in love would find time to write..."

It was ten o'clock when she closed her eyes.

At that same moment in far away Spain, Lord Wellington sent the Light and 4th Divisions charging through dank mists into a hell of hundreds of exploding powder barrels, shells, grenades, and the glittering *chevaux de frise* that protected the ramparts of the defiant city of Badajoz. By morning, the dead lay piled thick in the breaches, and hundreds of Britain's finest young men hung impaled on the sturdy beams bristling with spikes and sword blades that had been thrown up to halt their advance. The slaughter was appalling, and upon learning he had lost almost five thousand men, even the iron control of my Lord Wellington broke, and he wept.

CHAPTER THREE

ON MONDAY HELENA'S STRUGGLES to avert financial disaster occupied her mind to the exclusion of all else. Rack her brains as she would, however, she could think of no one to whom to turn, except her Uncle Tobias or Viscount Burtonbrook. A corner of her mind told her she had a right to appeal to the head of the family of which she would soon be a part, but her every instinct quailed from such an action. Lord Burtonbrook was, as her brothers would say, so very high in the instep, and she was only a *promised* bride. What a horrid way to preface her married life—to have to borrow from Robert's family!

By late afternoon she had reached a decision: if things became desperate she must go to Curzon Street. If she was sufficiently clever with her words, she might obtain his lordship's aid without even having to beg for it. Sighing heavily, she rose from the small escritoire in her chamber, and only then became aware that there was a deal of confusion in the street. She hurried to open the window. People were gathered in little knots on the flagway, and several gentlemen were shouting and waving a newspaper. Something of great importance must have happened. Perhaps the poor king had died and the newly appointed Regent had already acceded to the throne.

Emmett, who had gone for a walk with Mama, came racing down the street in obvious excitement. Helena ran to the stairs. She was almost to the downstairs hall when the front door burst open and her brother sprinted inside. His eyes blazing, he took off his hat and flung it in the air. "Hurrah for Lord Wellington!" he shouted breathlessly. "There has been a great battle! Badajoz has fallen—at last! Hurrah!"

Mrs. Vernon and the maids were loud in their patriotic joy. Helena had to shout to make herself heard. "Emmett—where is Mama?"

"She stayed to talk to the neighbours. People are in a great state, I can tell you! Is it not marvellous? Talavera; Bussaco; Albuera; Ciudad Rodrigo—and now Badajoz! Our Wellington is squashing old Boney at every turn! Come out and hear all the church bells! We've won! We've won!"

There was much celebrating that evening, with impromptu victory parties held in countless homes. Mrs. Hammond was in the highest spirits, and Helena was as joyful as she could be with the shadow of Newgate lurking always at the back of her mind. She had found it difficult to sleep these past few nights, and retired early. She had no sooner blown out her candle and lain down however, than the shouts of a newspaper vendor brought her sitting bolt upright, her eyes huge with a new terror.

"Late News Special! Latest News! Heavy casualties at Badajoz! Thousands dead! Heavy casualties!"

Once again, Helena passed a restless night.

THE NATION WAS in a holiday mood and there was little concern expressed over the enormous loss of life. Such losses were to be expected in warfare, especially against a town so inured to siege as Badajoz. Only those whose loved ones had fought and of whom there was as yet no word were haunted by fear of what the next post might bring.

On Thursday of that interminable week, Miss Savage paid a morning call to the small house off Fitzroy Square. She was paler than usual, but she asked kindly if there was word of Captain Eastleigh or the Hammond brothers, all of whom had fought with the Light Division. Helena had no news, and the two girls decided to walk to Curzon Street to see what might be learned from Lord Burtonbrook.

The viscount was at home and received his young callers graciously. He looked drawn and sombre, and said he had no word of his grand-nephew but that a number of the sons of his friends had been "knocked down." He reeled off the names of many of Britain's finest families, and Helena gave a little exclamation when a familiar one was included.

His lordship paused, looking at her enquiringly. "You know Peter Cliveden?"

She felt cold and replied, "Very slightly, sir. He rescued my youngest brother after a stagecoach accident at Christmastime. Is he killed?"

"I suspect so. We know he was hit and fell from one of the first scaling ladders." For once, strong emotion was reflected in the austere face. He said sadly, "Pity. He was a fine boy." A moment later, he terminated the interview, promising to send word the instant he heard anything.

On the way back to Fitzroy Square the friends said little. It was the first time the war had touched Helena so closely. She had a sudden memory of Lieutenant Cliveden, sitting in the kitchen while she'd bathed his wrist. How young he had been . . . and with such nice smiling eyes, even if he was a—

Geraldine said in an odd voice, "Helena, is that not your brother?"

A closed carriage, its door wide open, stood outside the little red brick house. A tall broad shouldered army officer was walking slowly down the front steps, talking to a dapper gentleman in civilian clothes. "Kayne!" cried Helena, with a joyous leap of the heart. In the next instant she noticed that the civilian carried a leather bag, and with a pang of fear she thought, 'He is a doctor!' "Mama?" she whispered, and started to run, Geraldine keeping pace with her.

As they passed the great Chalfont mansion, Lady Chalfont herself came out onto the porch, and called, "If we can be of any service, Miss Hammond . . ." Helena nodded an acknowledgement. This must be very bad indeed.

In another second she was clasped in her brother's strong arms. Kayne hugged her crushingly, then put her from him, and gazed gravely into her frightened face. She thought inconsequently, 'He looks older.' Then he was saying gently, "I cannot stay, love. I am sure you know there has been an action." He led her towards the house, Geraldine following silently. "I have brought despatches, and was allowed to escort some wounded officers home."

Helena gave a gasp, gripping his arm tighter and looking up at him, unable to say a word.

Kayne nodded. "Yes, my dear. It's Rostyn. You must be brave now..."

Shaking, she heard an odd little sound. Kayne released her, and with a startled exclamation, whipped around. Geraldine Savage had fainted dead away.

"WELL," EXCLAIMED HELENA indignantly. "If ever I saw a more disgraceful mess!"·

Rostyn lifted a thin but merry face, and grinned at her unrepentantly. Geraldine began to shoo cats from his bed, and rising from a comfortable if rather shabby chair, Savage drawled, "We had built a fine card house, Miss Hammond, but The Mushroom encroached, and spread it to the four winds!"

"And to the four corners of the room," Helena observed with a twinkle.

Savage scanned the pretty golden cat, and The Mushroom paused at her toilette to watch with much interest the dangling ribbon of his quizzing glass. "The wretched animal don't even look slightly intimidated," complained Savage, "though I distinctly warned it I should wring its scrawny—"

"'Ware!" cried Rostyn.

Savage gave a yelp, and swung the quizzing glass aside. Unhappily, The Mushroom—no lightweight— had already obtained a fang and claw grip on the ribbon, and for a minute Savage was (as he later indignantly claimed) in imminent danger of being strangled. The resultant debacle reduced Rostyn to tears of laughter, which in turn brought a happy glow to Helena's eyes.

When peace was restored, she helped a still-giggling Geraldine gather up the remaining cards. Despite Savage's lurid threats against The Mushroom, she could only be grateful to him. He and his sister had been frequent visitors through this past week, their presence never failing to cheer her brother.

Rostyn had been on the fringes of a great mine explosion in the breaches of Badajoz. Only a few of those in the vicinity had survived the blast, and in addition to the wounds inflicted by flying steel fragments, Rostyn had been hurled seventy yards and his spine so damaged that it was feared he might never walk again. When Kayne had first brought him home he'd been such a mass of bandages that poor Mrs. Hammond had taken one look at him and collapsed, afterwards being confined to her bed for three days. Helena had put financial worries aside while she cared for her loved ones. At first, Rostyn had been too weak and ill to do more than sleep, but his was a fighting spirit, and he had rallied so well that the doctor now described his progress as excellent.

"The Mushroom heard you threaten her, you see Leo," he said, as his sister smoothed the pillows. "Are you come to chase my guests away, Nell?"

"To the contrary, love. I have come to invite them to stay for luncheon, if they can spare the time."

Geraldine said without hesitation that she would be delighted to stay, but her brother declared himself too terrified to remain, then laughingly admitted a prior engagement.

Helena walked downstairs with him. "You both are too good to us," she said warmly. "I had feared you might think it improper for Gerry to remain in my brother's bedchamber, although—under the circumstances—"

"The circumstances of her being in love with him?" he drawled.

She hesitated. "I had rather thought she was. How sad, that he is now scarce a—a suitable candidate for her hand."

"And what of the candidate for *your* hand, ma'am? Surely you must have heard something by now?"

Aware of the deliberate evasion and caught off guard, she blushed painfully and could not meet his eyes as he handed her down the last stair. "I have heard nothing, Mr. Savage."

He gave a muffled snort. "And do you say that Burtonbrook ain't heard nothing either? Come now, ma'am—he's a power. He must know *something* of Eastleigh. 'Tis nigh two weeks since Badajoz fell."

She forced herself not to be offended by his sarcasm. "I have felt once or twice that—that his lordship knows something, and cannot bring himself to tell me." She bit her lip, tears smarting under her eyelids.

Watching that distressed but lovely face, Savage squeezed her small hand and said in an offhand way that he'd go and have a word with the "old curmudgeon" and if he learned anything would call back later in the day.

Helena stood on the steps for a moment, looking after him, still not quite knowing what to make of so complex a nature. She was turning back into the house when a luxurious barouche swept around the corner, slowed, and halted at the kennel. The footman sprang down to open the door, let down the step, and assist the occupant to alight. This was evidently a rather difficult task, and reaching the flagway at last, the gentleman paused as though wearied, and leaned heavily on a cane. He glanced up, saw the slim girl, and at once took off his beaver hat, and advanced alone.

Helena stared in astonishment. The young officer who had rescued Emmett four months ago, wore civilian dress and looked gaunt and ill. There were dark shadows around the grey eyes, but if those eyes held a faint strained look of pain, there was also an eagerness that touched her heart. "Why, Mr. Cliveden," she exclaimed, going down the steps to meet him. "How very glad I am to see you! We had heard you were—"

"Dead, I fancy," he said rather breathlessly. "Not quite, ma'am."

She longed to offer her aid as he struggled doggedly up the six rather steep steps to the front door, but he managed somehow, and she led him to the morning room, apologizing for its rather untidy appearance. "We are going to convert it to a bedchamber for my brother," she explained, "so that he will be able to get about more easily when he has his invalid chair."

At her insistence Cliveden sank onto a sofa, looking so white and pinched about the nostrils that Helena's heart thundered for fear he was about to collapse at her feet. She hurried to pour a glass of brandy, and after he had sipped it gratefully, a faint colour returned to his thin face.

Sitting near him, she said gently, "I am so sorry you were wounded. You have left the army, I see. Are you sure you are well enough to be out?"

Surprising her, he answered candidly, "Probably not, ma'am. But I had to come." Watching her closely, he went on in a troubled way, "You *have* been told about—about poor Eastleigh?"

The sudden and complete pallor of her bewitching face was his answer.

One hand fluttered to her throat. She whispered, "No. Nothing. I beg you will n-not hesitate, sir. I think I know what—you have to tell me."

Agitated, he struggled to his feet. "Dear ma'am, I cannot tell you how I regret to be the one to break it to you, but—er—"

The room seemed to have become full of grey mist. Helena heard her own voice, astoundingly steady, but very far away. "He is killed, is he not?"

A pause, then a reluctant, "Miss Hammond—I am so sorry..."

MRS. WINIFRED HAMMOND had been a semi-invalid since Rostyn had been brought home, but Fate's latest hammer blow reacted powerfully upon her. She rallied at once and began to bustle about with unparalleled vigour, running the household, comforting her shattered daughter, chattering with her son whenever Miss Savage was not present to help keep that gentleman company.

For two days Helena was so lost in grief she could do no more than keep to her bed and strive to muffle her sobs, but despite her heartbreak and the crushing sense of irreparable loss, the news had not come as a complete surprise. The long silence had of itself to some extent prepared her, besides which she had suspected that Lord Burtonbrook knew more than he admitted. These facts, added to her knowledge of how desperately she was needed, enabled her to at least outwardly compose herself and take up her usual tasks.

If she had but known it, her valiant effort to control and conceal her sorrow was more painful for her family than her tears had been. Straightening Rostyn's pillows one warm afternoon, Mrs. Hammond said in a near snarl, "That vicious viscount! From what Cliveden said, dear Lord Robert was slain at the height of the battle. Certainly Lord Ajax must have been notified, yet he had not the decency to tell my poor child, but sat there glooming in silence, and let that poor wounded boy drag himself here with the sad news."

Rostyn, guarding himself against her violent movements, enquired, "Have you seen his mightiness, Mama?"

"Small chance! I went to pay a call, and the knocker was off the door, and the porter yawning in my face and telling me his lordship has removed to his Scottish estates! *Retreated* is what he should have said! Run away for fear he might be called upon to—" She cut off her words quickly, plumping the pillow so vi-

olently that Rostyn pointed out aggrievedly that it was
unkind to box the ears of a wounded veteran.

On that same afternoon, Helena sat alone in the
morning room reading three letters that had been delivered by the postman. The first of these was a re-
gretful notification that since Mrs. Hammond was
now almost nine months in arrears with Master Emmett Hammond's fees, his continuance at Harrow was
not possible and unless payment in full was received
by the end of the term he would not be readmitted in
the autumn. Also, it would be necessary "to take
steps." Shivering, Helena read no further, but broke
the seals on the next letter. This was from Messrs.
Stevenson and Bush, Grocers, and was couched in less
polite terms. The unpaid balance on Mrs. George
Hammond's account had now reached the sum of
fifty-three pounds, ten shillings and fourpence. Mrs.
Hammond having ignored repeated requests for payment, Messrs. Stevenson and Bush had no alternative
but to institute execution proceedings. Helena gave a
scared little whimper. That meant some horrid rough
Bailiff would arrive at any moment and move into the
house to ensure they not remove any furniture or
valuables prior to their being auctioned off for payment of debts! "Oh, my *Lord*!" she whispered.
"What*ever* am I to do?" The third letter, in much the
same vein as the second, was from the coal merchant,
his bill amounting to forty pounds, which was to be
paid "*By Return*. PLEASE!!"

Helena was still staring numbly at those three ominous sheets of paper, when Mrs. Hammond came into
the room, chattering brightly of Rostyn's marked im-

provement. Something in her daughter's expression
sent her glance to the letters. Her busy words ceased
as she took them up, and she turned very pale. "Oh,
my love," she faltered. "I am so very sorry about dear
Lord Robert, truly I am. And heaven forfend that I
should criticize. But—I cannot help but wonder why
he must get into such a dreadful battle when he *knew*
how badly we needed him. Only look at the pickle he
has left us, for who is to pay Emmett's expenses
now?"

Helena gazed at the mother she had always loved so
deeply. Dainty and loving and generous was Mama.
And with not one single particle of common sense,
bless her. But how carefree and happy had been their
childhood; how many memories of fun and shared
laughter; how deep the bonds that bound them. And
so she found a smile somehow, and hugging the exas-
perating little lady fondly, said, "Never worry, dearest. I think I know just the man."

MR. LEOPOLD SAVAGE BLINKED at the enchanting
loveliness of the girl who sat so still in the red velvet
chair in his sunny study. His rooms on Sackville Street
were elegantly appointed and spacious. He had entertained many ladies here, but never had one arrived in
broad daylight, attended only by a maid. Her pale
green satin redingote with the dark green braid trim,
and the modified poke of her matching green silk
bonnet with the white plumes curling saucily over the
brim became her so admirably that his breath had actually been taken away when first he saw her waiting
for him. He had been mildly surprised that she was not

in black gloves, but certainly never had he received a lady with more pleasure, nor been more taken aback by her reason for calling.

For once abandoning his bored air, he gasped out, "*Want* you dear Miss Helena? By Gad, but I do! Only—it's—er, a trifle sudden, ain't it?"

"You knew," said Helena, fighting to keep her voice steady, "that my—That Lord Robert Eastleigh fell at—at Badajoz?"

"I heard but three days since, ma'am. But don't you think you should allow a little time to—er...Well, that is—"

Helena lifted reproachful brown eyes to meet his startled blue ones. "You *said*, Mr. Savage, that you would be willing to take Eastleigh's place."

"Yes, I did say that. And I would...only..." Savage took a turn about the room, and recovering his sangfroid, paused to look down at her. "My dear," he said with his twisted smile, "I will be very honest. When I made that remark it was made to—ah, to you...*only*."

Sparks flashed in her eyes. She said bluntly, "And I am far less attractive now that I have a crippled brother to provide for."

Mr. Savage had the grace to wince a little, but murmured, "And a mother, and another brother who is rather a er—continuing charge. And," he shuddered, "those repulsive cats! I fear you would want them all to live with us. No, really my dear, you cannot know how this pains me, but—I *could* not!"

Helena felt as though the ground had been snatched away from beneath her feet. Her last hope was gone.

But whatever else, he was no hypocrite; he had been open with her and he spoke truth. Crushed, she gave no sign of it, but stood, her little chin well up. "I see. I hope you are not offended."

He thought she had never looked more pathetically brave and desirable. He said ardently, "Dear lady, I adore you. May I offer another solution?"

With a renewal of hope Helena gazed intently into the blue eyes that seemed so earnest now.

"There is," he went on, "a very charming apartment just below this one. I would be most proud to redecorate it in any way you might wish and install you there. I would, of course, pay all your personal expenses. I might even manage Emmett's fees. You and I, my sweetness, could be so—" He paused then, reading correctly the rage in her narrowed eyes and flushed cheeks. "Do not reply too quickly," he warned. "You are exquisite, but I think you will not find any gentleman willing to take on *all* your obligations."

"Had you and Geraldine not been so kind to us, Mr. Savage," said Helena through her teeth, "I should box your ears! I was wrong to come here, I know, but I did not rate that insult from a gentleman I believed to be a friend. For shame sir!" She marched to the door and flung it open while he stood there slightly frowning at her.

Turning back, head high and eyes blazing, she ignored the hovering footman, and said ringingly, "I shall bring us about somehow, Mr. Savage, but I am not yet so destitute as to be obliged to accept a slip on

the shoulder from you, or any other man! Good day
to you, sir!''

His face very red, Leopold Savage met the footman's goggle-eyed stare and hurled a small covered
porcelain jar at him.

He missed. The jar, which chanced to be full of his
new blend of snuff, struck the door jamb and re-
bounded. Which was unfortunate.

BY THE TIME HELENA reached Fitzroy Square her
brisk walk had slowed to little more than a saunter,
and her spirits had sunk to the point she could scarcely
keep back the tears. Rostyn was so young, with so
much of life still before him, and he had always been
so sporting mad. It seemed bitterly unfair that he
should be doomed to an invalid chair for the rest of his
days. He was trying so hard to be brave and cheerful,
but whatever would become of him if she could not
find a way to provide? What would become of all of
them? Dear Kayne was sending home most of his pay,
and together with what she had obtained from selling
her few pieces of antique jewellery and the diamond
bracelet Lord Robert had given her, she'd managed to
hold their creditors at bay. Until now. Uncle Tobias
had been so good, and he would probably help to
some extent if she appealed to him, but he had his own
large family to consider, and, although he lived well as
befitted a retired General of the Army, he was not so
rich he could pay off all mama's debts and take care of
them indefinitely. She shouldn't have been so cowardly about approaching Lord Burtonbrook, but it
was too late now; his lordship had left Town, and

whatever claim she may once have had upon him was
no more. She had no great fears for herself; she could
find work as a governess—perhaps even manage to
support Mama in a room somewhere. But how to keep
Emmett at school, or provide the care Rostyn
needed . . .

The maid, who had been discreetly silent all the way
home, said, "We have a caller, miss."

A carriage was drawn up outside; a familiar carriage. Mr. Cliveden had called again. How kind, when
it was so painful for him to get about. He'd probably
come to see how Rostyn went on.

Mrs. Vernon opened the door before she knocked.
"I been watching for you, Miss Nell," she whispered.
"That poor Lieutenant Cliveden is waiting in the
withdrawing room. Your mama is taking a little nap
and he'd not let me disturb her."

The lieutenant was seated by the empty hearth, his
head leaning back against the chair. At first Helena
thought he was asleep, but he heard her step and at
once opened his eyes, took up his cane and struggled
to his feet.

She hurried to offer her hand, then sat down
quickly, urging him to do the same. "How very kind
of you to call, sir. Have you seen my brother?"

"No, ma'am." He gestured to the cane with a rueful grin. "Stairs are a touch difficult for me just now."

She nodded sympathetically. "It is the right leg that
is the trouble, I think? I had heard you were shot. Is
that—where . . . ?"

"Yes. But—" he gave an impatient gesture. "I
won't take up your time with all that. The thing is . . . I

know the news I had for you on my last visit was distressing in the extreme." He watched her face anxiously, angered by the faint suggestion of despair that her polite calm could not hide. "You were—deeply attached to Lord Eastleigh, ma'am?" She was faintly irritated. Whatever did he think? "Yes. He was—" It was difficult to keep her voice from quavering. "He was—"

"A splendid fellow," he inserted hurriedly. "Yes. He saved my life, you know."

"No, I didn't know that. Would it be painful for you to tell me how?"

He hesitated, staring rather blindly at First Cat who had wandered in and was inspecting his cane. "It was during our first advance. The defences were incredible. They sent hundreds of exploding powder barrels down on us..." His voice faded, his eyes briefly reflecting horror. Almost immediately, he recovered himself and said in a firmer tone, "Anyway, when I was knocked off the ladder, a lancer thought me fair game. Eastleigh made short work of him, but as he was trying to haul me off, he was hit."

Helena put a trembling hand over her eyes and Cliveden watched her through a short silence. "I would not be here," he went on, his voice rather harsh, "had it not been for poor Bob. If the notion is not repugnant to you, Miss Hammond, I would like to do what I can to fill the gap he left. To—er, to try and finish what he was unable to accomplish. As it—er, were."

Helena lowered her hand and stared at him. "Mr. Cliveden, perhaps you do not know, but we are very deep in debt."

"I think I have some grasp of your—financial difficulties, ma'am."

"You do? Then do you say you are prepared to advance us a loan?"

He struggled to his feet and stood before her, his thin face very white, and an odd, scared look in the shadowed grey eyes. "No, ma'am. I want to provide for your future. But—to have that right, I must ask the honour of your—" he gulped, and finished with a rush "—of your hand in marriage."

"Good heavens!" gasped Helena. "But you scarcely know me. Or I you!"

"I know that you are good, and kind, and—er, gentle." He flushed, and stammered on, "You are very beautiful, ma'am, and I know also that you must have many suitors. But, I am a wealthy man. I can offer you a good enough house in town, and I've a very nice place in Sussex which your family might find agreeable, and where it might be pleasant for your brother to convalesce. We would likely spend most of the year there, for I'm not much one for the ton and its nonsense. And your cats would be welcome, for we are—er, quite plagued with mice. And rats," he added reinforcingly.

"Mr. Cliveden," said Helena, overwhelmed. "So far all you have said is what *you* have to offer *me*. Has it not occurred to you that I have nothing to offer you in return? My heart was given to another. Irrevocably." It seemed to her that he swayed a little, and she besought him to sit down again. When he had done so with a barely audible sigh of relief, she said with gentle but impeccable honesty, "I cannot love again, sir. Not ever."

"No, of course not. I—er, would not expect— Well, as you said, we scarce know each other."

"But sir, this is not equitable surely? You must—" her eyes fell, and she knew she was blushing "—you must want an heir?"

"No, no!" he said vehemently. And as her eyes lifted to his in astonishment, he floundered, "Well, I do, of course. But—not right away. I mean, er—well, as you see ma'am, I'm considerably disabled and my doctor tells me I shall be for quite some time. I should not force myself upon—Ah, you would be unmolested, Miss Hammond. Unless you—er, should ever wish . . ." Very red now, he gulped, "Wish—otherwise."

She had to fight a smile, but she was touched. "You are willing to do this out of your sense of obligation to my late fiancé. I honour you for that loyalty. But, Mr. Cliveden, it would be too unfair. You are a young man, and I feel sure will soon recover from your injuries. You will want to find someone with whom you could share tenderness. A—a loving relationship."

"I have," he blurted.

Her lower lip sagged. She echoed feebly, "You *have*? Then, why not marry the lady you—"

"Because I cannot, ma'am. She's rankly ineligi—" He broke off with a groan. "Oh, Lord! I don't mean that. But, my father has told me flat out that he will disinherit me if I wed Miss Grey. So we have—" he dragged out his handkerchief and mopped his perspiring brow. "Er, taken other steps."

"You mean," she said, her eyes very wide, "that you have set her up as your mistress."

He bit his lip. "Y-yes, ma'am. I know it must sound disgraceful, but we are too devoted to part, and it seemed the only way. So I'd not be—I mean you'd not have to feel obliged to—ah—"

Helena looked away quickly. "I see," she said.

It sounded a much better arrangement than she could have expected of Leopold Savage, who she was very sure would never have agreed to such a Platonic relationship. Besides, whatever he may lack in the way of valour, she rather liked this shy young man, and if he was as wealthy as he implied, she would have achieved both a creditable match and a way out of their crushing debts. He did not really want this, that was obvious, poor fellow. He was so pale, and looked ready to faint, but he clearly felt duty bound to provide for the lady of the man who had given his life to save him. She experienced a devastating pang of sorrow. Dear brave Robert...Forcing grief away, she said, "Mr. Cliveden, I am very sure that Lord Eastleigh would not have wished that you feel so bound. I urge you to take time to think."

"I have taken time, ma'am. I've scarce thought of anything else since I learned— For the past three weeks. Miss Hammond, circumstances compel me to hasten. Have I your permission to speak to your Mama?"

"This is not at all proper," she said worriedly. "We should wait until we know each other better. I should pretend to be undecided. But—" she smiled at him gratefully. "I cannot refuse your very kind and noble offer, Mr. Cliveden. You have my permission."

CHAPTER FOUR

"IT ALL SEEMS DASHED havey-cavey to me." Comfortably, if inconveniently disposed upon a chaise longue in the downstairs hall, where he could see most of what went on and was in everybody's way, Rostyn moved aside the golden tail which waved before his eyes, and grumbled to its owner that he'd "never seen such a scramblement" in all his days. "A month ago, she didn't hardly know this fellow." The Mushroom had been so named because her coat was a rich honey gold and she had most unusual blue eyes, wherefore Emmett had said she was smug and conceited. She did not respond to Rostyn's remark, but considered him her property, and made occasional swipes at anyone passing too closely.

"Miss Helena is a married lady now," said Mrs. Vernon, bustling past carrying a large pile of lace tablecloths.

"If you could call that furtive fling a marriage ceremony," he called after her, then laughed as she was obliged to turn back, The Mushroom having captured a trailing end of lace with the result that three tablecloths were dislodged.

"Horrid brute," said Mrs. Vernon without rancour, and ejected the cat from the end of the chaise so that she might sit and rearrange her burdens.

Secretly pleased to have a little non-feline company, Rostyn continued his criticism. "Why the unseemly haste, is what I want to know."

"Now, Mr. Ross," soothed the housekeeper. "You know Mr. Cliveden's doctor ordered him into the country."

"Then let the fellow go! I do not see why we all must abandon town just because Helena has been swept off her feet by a man who is a frustrated martinet. I little dreamed when he brought my brother home last Christmas that I'd soon have him ordering my affairs! And—"

"Poor dear." Helena came in at the front door followed by two lackeys wearing the rich blue Cliveden livery, and carrying covered baskets. "Mrs. Vernon will show you where to put those," she advised these minions, then took the place the housekeeper had vacated and smiled at her red-faced brother. "Have we put you quite out of temper, Ross?"

"No," he said, embarrassed. "Shouldn't have said that. Only, I do not see why Mama and I cannot stay here."

"Because the country air will be good for you, love. Cliveden says—"

"Cliveden says! I'm damned sick of hearing that, if you want to know it. 'Cliveden says—' and we are all rushed through a nuptial as though we sought to keep it secret. 'Cliveden says—' and we are evicted from our home and whisked off into the hinterland,

miles from everywhere, or anyone we know, and—
Which reminds me," he interrupted himself rather too
nonchalantly. "Why don't Miss Geraldine and Savage come any more? Are they gone away, too?"

"I believe Geraldine did say they would spend a
month in Brighton. But not until the end of the Season, I think. You know how social minded Mr. Savage is, and with all the balls and routs and assemblies
that—"

"That I would have thought a newly married pair
would wish to attend," he put in sharply. "Instead of
slinking off to some remote cow byre!"

Helena looked away guiltily. "I think you forget
that Cliveden is recuperating from wounds, even as
you are, dearest."

He flushed again. "Yes. I am being a clod, I know."

"I say, Hammond," panted Cliveden, limping in
from the front steps and waving a sheaf of papers.
"Since you're at the heart of things, as it were, I wonder could you attend to these matters? They're your
mama's lists of Things That Must Not be Forgot, and
which creature is to go in which basket—they're all
numbered by the way, but she seems to have come up
two baskets short—and who is to travel in which carriage, et cetera. Too much for me."

Rostyn took the papers grudgingly, and was very
soon issuing commands like a Roman emperor, and
feeling quite useful again.

The journey to Sussex commenced on May Day,
and at nine o'clock their lengthy cavalcade began to
wind through the Spring morning, blessed by a glory
of blue sky and sunshine. Three coaches full of ser-

vants took the lead, followed by the luxurious travelling carriage conveying Mrs. Hammond and Rostyn,
and after that, Cliveden's equally luxurious barouche
in which rode the bride and groom. Next came four
more coaches packed with valuables, clothing, and
personal belongings. At the very end was a carter's
waggon in which were twelve very noisy baskets and
the gardener's boy who was to care for the occupants
en route. Mrs. Hammond had dithered over the dis-
position of the cats for some time, being disturbed by
the notion that two of them might not really belong to
her, but not sure which two were suspect. She was inclined to think Windy Wallets, who had such a pierc-
ing yowl, had wandered uninvited into the fold, but
could not reject him "because, he is so *odd* looking,
poor fellow. No one would ever give him a home."
Last but not least, several outriders roved the length
of the cavalcade to discourage highwaymen and others of their ilk from attempting to lighten the laden
vehicles.

They wound their way through the bustling cla-
mour of the city, the length of their train and the uproar from the waggon arousing a good deal of interest,
amusement, and not a few ribald suggestions. Helena
was engrossed in the ever changing fascinations beyond the window, especially along the Thames. When
they approached the magnificence of Westminster
Bridge, she turned eagerly to her husband to remark
on the wonder of it. Cliveden was asleep. She watched
him, still scarcely able to believe that she was really
married to this quietly unremarkable gentleman.

These past ten days had fairly raced by, with endless details to be attended to, among which there was the marriage announcement to be made; a special licence to be obtained; the complicated marriage contract to be drawn up; bride clothes purchased; wedding gifts acknowledged; arrangements made for much of the clothing and the larger articles of furniture to be packed and shipped by Pickford's; the Hammond debts attended to; and the deeply mortgaged little house off Fitzroy Square to be disposed of. Rostyn knew nothing of the last two matters, and she wondered in some anxiety what his eventual reaction would be. There could be no doubt but that the pressures of the hasty wedding had irritated him; his brave acceptance of his helpless state had given way to a querulous complaining quite unlike him, and yet she and Mama had agreed it would be dangerous to let him know how desperate had been their straits before Cliveden had offered this most unexpected and fortuitous lifeline.

Perhaps because of all the hurry and confusion, Helena's grief for her slain suitor had eased a little, and although at night her pillow was often wet with tears, she was occasionally startled to realize that she had been so swept up by the wedding plans that for an entire day she'd not so much as thought of Lord Robert.

She had become Mrs. Peter Cliveden two days ago; the wedding a quiet one with very few guests. It had been an ordeal none the less, for it could not fail to remind her of the blissful ceremony she'd expected to share with Lord Robert. Cliveden had behaved properly but without enthusiasm, and battling the ache in her heart Helena had guessed that he, too, was likely yearning for the lady he loved. His energy and vitality, less than a month after having been seriously wounded, had amazed her. When she'd spoken of it to Rostyn his only comment had been a scornful grunt. This was so unlike her usually generous brother that she'd wondered if her mention of Cliveden's remarkable recovery had seemed to Rostyn a criticism of his own far less rapid progress.

From the church they had gone directly to Cliveden House, the great mansion off the Strand, which had so awed her when she first had entered its magnificence. An army of servants, supervised by a major domo whose efficiency frightened her, had prepared a delicious wedding breakfast for the fifty guests. The bridegroom however had become ever more quiet and withdrawn until his pallor had caused Helena to fear he had overtaxed his strength and she had uttered her first wifely command—that he go at once to his bedchamber and rest. A twinkle had come into his tired eyes; he had done as commanded, but not before rather ostentatiously kissing her on the cheek much to the delight of the company. She had not seen him again until she'd sought her own chamber that evening and had been quite startled when he came into the room without knocking, clad in his night rail. Her maids had fled, giggling. Cliveden had crossed to where she sat at her dressing table rigid with fright, and kissed the back of her neck. As soon as the door closed he had murmured an apology. "But we must not allow the servants to suspect our—er, under-

standing you know, Mrs. Cliveden.'' He had stayed
with her for almost an hour, chatting easily, and so
restoring her shredded nerves that they had soon been
chuckling together over the humorous aspects of their
rush into matrimony.

Now, scanning the finely chiselled features, the
rather wistful droop to the mouth relaxed in sleep, she
found herself wondering who was his inamorata; what
she was like; whether she was pretty and kind.

Soon the carriage was rumbling over the bridge. The
mighty span had only been completed sixty-two years
ago, and was said to be one of the most beautiful
bridges in the world. It was crowded with pedestrians
and every kind of vehicle, which must surely consti-
tute a very great weight. Transferring her gaze to the
sparkling spread of the river, with its endless flow of
boats and barges, Helena wished Cliveden could share
the sight with her. She turned quickly and caught him
watching her with the strangest expression. It was gone
before she had properly identified it, and he murmured, "They are said to have used twice as much
Portland stone as was needed to build St. Paul's, did
you know?"

She confessed her ignorance. "If you are always so
informative, sir, I shall hope you can stay awake and
instruct me on our long journey."

"My apologies. Truly I am most remiss in the du-
ties of a bridegroom." He sat straighter and drawled
with a smile, "But I believe you can instruct *me* on
several points, madam wife. For instance, have you
a—er, fondness for Leopold Savage?"

It was so unexpected that she gave a shocked gasp. "Certainly not!"

"Dear me! I appear to have made a proper *faux pas*. Yet he was a frequent caller at your house, no? And he told me once that he admired you greatly."

"Hah!" snorted Helena, but noting a sudden narrowing of the grey eyes, she added hurriedly, "His sister, Geraldine, and I were at Seminary together, and I must own that both she and Mr. Savage were very kind to my brother during his illness."

"But Savage has annoyed you, I perceive. Must I call him out, ma'am?"

He said it calmly enough, yet there was an edge to his voice that she had not heard before. Still, it was silly to imagine a menace from this mild-mannered gentleman, and her musical little laugh rang out. "I wish you will not. Surely you have had enough of fighting for a while?"

The remark brought an inevitable reminder of the great battle, and her eyes became saddened until Cliveden began to speculate on the possible ownership of the two extra cats, and to ask her with great pseudo-anxiety whether they might have committed theft by bringing the animals with them.

Partly because they carried two invalids, and partly because of the basketed felines, their progress was not rapid. To permit the shortest possible incarceration of the animals, Cliveden had arranged that another waggon driver await them at The Bull and Bottle in Redhill. The weather was clear and warm and a full moon would enable the waggon to continue on to Sussex, which Cliveden estimated it would reach at about midnight. The rest of the train would pass the night at the old inn. As arranged, the waggoneer was waiting. Mrs. Hammond rushed to console her pets and reassure each individually that they would soon arrive at their lovely new home in the country where dozens of mice and rats waited to be caught.

The hostelry exuded comfort, and a pleasant suite awaited Helena. She was again briefly apprehensive when Cliveden accompanied her into the bedchamber, but having assured himself that she would be comfortable, he left her and went away to his solitary room.

Next morning, they turned to the southeast. The North Downs were left behind, and they took luncheon at a large and spotless farmhouse outside Tunbridge Wells, where Cliveden was welcomed as if he was royalty, and the bride was exclaimed over with many looks of envy from the maids (much to the bridegroom's delight). There was a private room where the ladies could rest and refresh themselves, and Fulton, Cliveden's rather dour valet, took charge of Rostyn's invalid chair. Half an hour later they all enjoyed an excellent meal spread for them on a table looking out over a pretty garden.

By three o'clock they were in Sussex, the carriages following winding lanes fragrant with blossoms and dappled by warm sunlight. Helena had never been in The Weald, and was charmed by the lush greens of the rolling countryside threaded by its many streams and rivers; the neat hamlets and villages; the friendly smiles of the country folk. Soon, they turned onto a lane which climbed steadily uphill. They looked down

upon a quaint old village with a winding tree-lined
street of whitewashed thatched cottages grouped about
a tranquil pond. Helena peered about in delight.
"How very pretty and peaceful it is. Is your estate
nearby, Mr. Cliveden?"

"We have been on my—our lands this past ten
minutes, ma'am."

She gave a squeak of excitement. "Then that dear
little village belongs to you!"

"To us, Mrs. Cliveden. You shall see the house very
soon now."

The coaches stopped at the top of the hill, and
everyone climbed out, two footmen carrying Rostyn
into the sunshine.

Cliveden offered Helena his arm, but like a mis-
chievous small boy ignored her eager questions and
silently led the way to the brink of the hill.

She halted, and stood staring. "Oh," she murmured. "I think I never saw anything so lovely. Has
it a name?"

"It is called Whisperwood, and has been in my
family for almost four hundred years, although the
original block is now in ruins. From here you can
barely see it—just the chimneys at the back there,
amongst the trees. The present house was begun in
1679, and is quite modern." He obviously loved the
great house, and asked Mrs. Hammond, "What do
you think of it, ma'am?"

"It is very much larger than I had supposed," the
lady answered, scanning the sprawl of the distant two-
storied house, "and to keep it properly maintained

must require many servants. How many are on your staff, Cliveden?''

He looked startled and admitted he wasn't sure. ''Luckily, my steward handles such matters, but I believe there are in the neighbourhood of forty.''

Regarding the pastoral beauty spread below him, Rostyn's eyes were sullen. "One thing, Mama," he muttered. "It's big enough that you and I can keep out of the way of our two lovebirds."

Helena turned away quickly and walked closer to the downward slope. Coming up behind her, Cliveden said low-voiced, "He's near exhaustion, I think. This long journey has been hard on him, and he has more than his share of pride. He probably resents being summarily uprooted, and even more, resents being a helpless recipient of my charity."

He had misunderstood the reason for her distress, but she gave him a grateful smile. "You are very kind, sir."

"Oh no. But it is logical for such a man to feel so."

"Yes. And it is logical that you should be almost as tired as my brother. Let us go on, sir, so that you can rest."

The carriages were soon winding down the hill and across the floor of the shallow valley. The drive led through the drowsing quiet of a belt of well-thinned woodland where bluebells spread their azure carpet and primroses peeped in shy clusters amid the dappled shade. Emerging into the glory of the golden afternoon, they drove through a spacious park ending in a low balustrade beyond which were velvety emerald lawns, and flowerbeds brilliant with colour that looped about the buildings like jewelled necklaces. The house managed to look welcoming despite its size, the many gables along the front jutting at angles here and there, each embellished by its own intricately patterned half-timbering.

Helena became aware that Cliveden had said something in his quiet way, and she turned to him, her eyes very bright. "Oh! Your pardon, sir?"

He chuckled. "You really do like it."

"It is the loveliest house I ever saw," she said seriously.

"And you shall not mind living here for much of the year?"

"I think I would be very sad when the time came to leave it."

Much later, she was to remember those words.

HELENA FOUND THE INSIDE of Whisperwood as enchanting as the exterior. The rooms used by family and guests were all situated in the main block, while the backward slanting shorter wing, like the extended foot of a reclining letter L, contained the service areas and indoor servants' quarters. They entered the house through a bright hall, and came to a great central saloon that extended to the back, where French doors rich with stained glass gave onto a wide terrace and steps led down to more gardens and ornamental water. Limping along behind the two ladies, Cliveden groaned to find that First Cat had taken up residence atop the gilded harpsichord at one end of the saloon, and Delilah was industriously cleaning herself in a patch of sunlight on the book room reference table, with Soot and Fribble sharing the window seat. In the luxurious but comfortable withdrawing room The Mushroom was comfortably ensconced on a sofa. "I shall have to install some large and vicious dogs," said Cliveden thoughtfully.

"With big sharp teeth," laughed Helena, who was beginning to feel more at ease with him.

Rostyn was wheeled in, and a discreet individual who had been hovering to the background, led the way to a pleasant room at the northeast corner of the ground floor which had obviously been recently converted to a bedchamber. Glancing around at well-filled bookcases, a large tester bed, comfortable chairs, and ample chests and wardrobes, Rostyn said, "Jolly nice. Thank you Cliveden."

The words were as if torn from him, and Helena flinched, but if her husband noticed the harsh tone, he gave no sign. "Daniels will serve as your valet, for the time being, at least," he said amiably.

Daniels, who was tall and sturdily built, smiled at his new gentleman and indicated a wish to be of service, and the ladies left Rostyn to rest. Mrs. Hammond went off with Chartley, the elderly and distinguished butler, and Helena allowed her husband to lead her up the stairs while praying that Rostyn would soon recover his good humour.

The suite allocated to her was a dream of thick rugs and dainty furnishings, dominated by a great canopied bed with daringly flimsy curtains of cream silk embroidered with pastel flowers and tied back with pink satin ropes. The windows looked out over the front gardens and she could see the hill beyond which was the quaint village. The parlour was cosy with deep cushioned chairs, a fine Adam fireplace, and walls hung with several beautiful gilt-framed prints of country life. She had never known such a degree of elegance, and drifted about in a happy daze until Cliveden said he'd best change for dinner, and limped to a door on the far side of her parlour. His bedchamber must lie on the other side of that door! Shocked out of her delight, Helena stared, wide-eyed.

He turned back, one hand on the latch, and said apologetically, "I instructed most of my servants to stay out of sight until you are able to rest a little, but they are all agog to meet you and I'm afraid will be waiting to be presented when we go downstairs." He started away but again turned back. "Dash it, I keep forgetting you are my wife. Pray come and inspect my rooms. It would probably appear strange if you did not do so."

Considerably shaken by the perfectly logical proximity of their apartments, she followed him, but once inside curiosity got the better of her, and she looked about critically. His bedchamber it most certainly was, but she thought it might also have housed an indoor cricket match. It was a huge barn of a room, the furnishings of massive dark mahogany, the rugs a dull green, the great plaster chimney piece enlivened by writhing dragons and hideous gargoyles, and the bedcurtains and draperies a dreary maroon velvet. "Ugh," she exclaimed involuntarily.

Cliveden gave a shout of laughter. Turning to him, Helena's mortification was swept away. She had never seen him laugh like that, and for the first time com-

prehended why the damsels at the farmhouse had regarded her so enviously. Recovering her wits with an
effort, she faltered, "It is just that it looks so—echoing, and depressing."

"Then we must do away with the lot of it," he said,
still chuckling. "Not for the world would I have this
room appear to you in a bad light. It will be redeco-
rated to your tastes ma'am, for—who knows? Some
day, or night, you might feel inclined to stop in for a—
er, chat. Or something."

It seemed an odd remark in view of their arrangement, and scanning him narrowly Helena made some
discoveries about her spouse that she'd not had time
to notice during the frenetic pace of these busy days.
Firstly, he was no longer using his cane; and sec-
ondly, the hollows about his eyes were almost gone.
Also, the way he had of glancing at her from under his
brows, his mouth perfectly solemn, but with a twinkle in the grey eyes was most unsettling.

As GOOD AS HIS WORD Cliveden required his steward
to consult with his bride regarding the restoration of
the master bedchamber. Mr. Shafer was a big bluff
man whose amiability was matched by an enormous
garrulity. He was devoted to his young employer, and
proved to be as shrewd as he was large. Before the
week was out workmen were busy in the house. The
uproar was continuous, but when Rostyn grumbled at
breakfast one morning that he'd been woken at dawn
by all the thumpings and hammerings, Cliveden
drawled that it was as well. "You've been long enough
in bed. Time to be up and doing."

Rostyn glared at him. "Doing? What the devil am I able to do?"

Helena held her breath, and Mrs. Hammond looked at her handsome son in distress. Cliveden said with a bored shrug, "My dear fellow, if Michelangelo could spend more than four years painting the ceiling of the Sistine Chapel while lying on his back, I'd think a sturdy chap like you could do any number of things in an invalid chair. If you insist on clinging to the contrivance."

"Cliveden!" expostulated Helena angrily.

Rostyn all but spluttered with wrath, *"Clinging?"* he roared. "What—"

His impassioned defence was interrupted by a great outburst of yowls, howls, and shouts, capped by a high-pitched and sustained barking.

"Good Lord," muttered Cliveden, rising from the table. "Some misguided hound has blundered into this cat sanctuary."

The barking became a frenzied yelping. Before Cliveden could cross the breakfast parlour, the door burst open, and Emmett galloped in, grinning from ear to ear, and with a wailing beagle puppy clasped in his arms. He thrust the puppy at Cliveden and hurried to embrace his family. "Hello, Mama. Hello, Rostyn. Oh, you do look nice, Helena." Almost in the same breath, he turned to the silent Cliveden and added, "Jolly good of you to send your coachman to bring me here, sir. I hope it wasn't an inconvenience."

"He's used to Hammonds hanging on his coattails," sneered Rostyn.

"Oh, I shan't do that, don't worry sir," beamed Emmett, adding naively, "Can you take care of my dog, please? Turnip gave him a scratch on the beak."

"So I see," drawled Cliveden. "No, I most certainly cannot repair this. Take it." He tossed the whining dog at the boy and added, "I know little of veterinary matters. Your brother will help—he'll be glad to do something to earn his keep—eh, Hammond?"

He turned on his heel and left before the outraged Rostyn could recover sufficiently to give voice to his wrath, and was then obliged to restrain himself because his little brother was looking anxiously from one to the other of their variously shocked and angry faces.

"Have I done something wrong?" asked Emmett. "Should I not have come?"

"Of course you have done nothing wrong, dear," said his mother, exchanging a worried glance with her daughter. "Come and sit down and have some breakfast. Your brother will want to take your puppy to the kitchen I expect, and see what can be done for the poor creature. Was he chasing the cats, love? I fancy they've now taught him not to do so, which is just as well. Shall you like to spend the Long Vacation here? It is the loveliest . . ."

Her pleasant voice followed them as Helena wheeled Rostyn and his charge into the corridor. A soon as they were out of earshot of any of the servants, she said softly, "My dear, I am so sorry. I think he does not mean to be so abrupt."

"I think he is damnably top-lofty," snarled Rostyn. "He fancies me to be fudging, does he? Blast the fellow! If he did but know how I *hate* having to take his charity! I'd pay him every damned farthing if it was in my power. Not that it's so curst much. He got himself the prettiest girl in London, only because she was too lost in grief to withstand him."

Helena stopped the chair beside a marble bench and sat down facing him. "That is not true, Rostyn," she said with quiet dignity. "Cliveden came to our rescue when we were hopelessly—as you would say—under the hatches."

"Fustian! The beastly muckworm paid a few bills perhaps, but only because he wanted *you*! He can certainly afford a decent Settlement, and after all, what's so rare about—"

"He did *not* want me! He *does* not want me! And if you—"

He interrupted her with a harsh laugh. "God help you then if he ever *does* want you! I'm not blind, Nell. I've seen the way he looks at you. One might think he'd not have balked at paying a few duns."

"There were more than a few." Helena leant nearer and lowered her voice. "Mama had run out of funds long ago, Ross, and had a lovely time, bless her, in borrowing from everybody in sight. She was really surprised when it was suggested she should start paying them back."

He eyed her uneasily. "I think you are bamming. Who would have lent her money? Everyone knew we'd not a feather to fly with."

"Uncle Tobias at first. More recently, several moneylenders in the City. And she had mortgaged the house to the point that we were about to be evicted!"

Very pale now, he stared at her, then said a derisive, "Silly rubbish! What could she offer as security? Moneylenders don't—"

"To them, she offered my betrothal to Lord Burtonbrook's heir."

"Oh... Jupiter!"

"Yes, love. When poor Robert was killed we had already been notified that Emmett could not return to Harrow, and there was a Bailiff due in the house at any instant. I was able to put them off for a little while by selling my few scraps of decent jewellery."

He tensed and said angrily, "Now I *know* you're fudging, Helena! You wore grandmama's pearls only yesterday!"

"Yes, because Cliveden was so kind as to buy them back for me. No, don't say it was because he cares for me. He has another lady—of ineligible birth—but with whom he is deep in love. He offered for me because Eastleigh saved his life and was killed doing so."

His jaw dropped. "But—"

"He is an honourable gentleman, and felt obliged to fulfill Lord Robert's commitments. I accepted his offer because I was desperate. I simply did not know where to turn until he came and promised to pay all our debts. And because he also offered a *mariage de convenance*. In—er, in the fullest sense." She straightened, knowing her face was red, but looking steadily into his shocked eyes. "This is the 'beastly muckworm' you so despise, Ross."

He took a deep breath. "He is not repugnant to you?"

"No. Not in the slightest."

"But you do not love him? Not at all?"

She gave a sad smile. "How could I? My heart was given to Robert."

"In other words," he said fiercely, "you sold yourself to a man for whom you have no affection, so as to pay debts *I* should have shouldered!"

"Oh, Rostyn, why will you not see—"

"I see, all right! I see that I'm properly beholden to him, damn him!" He drove a clenched fist at the arm of his chair, startling the puppy who had fallen asleep. "I wish to God I might throw every last groat into his smug face! But—" he gave a stiff smile. "I cannot afford false pride, and must bow to him and offer my humble apologies." His lip curled. "Oh, don't look so alarmed, m'dear. I shall keep my tongue between my teeth, for I'm fairly trapped in his loathsome charity. But, by God you may be sure I shall bend every effort to—somehow—remove myself from his list of dependents!"

Helena sighed and took the grips of the invalid chair once more.

CHAPTER FIVE

WHETHER CLIVEDEN WAS STILL too weak to be inclined for *l'amour*, or the gloomy weather discouraged him, Helena could not tell, but not once during the days that followed did he depart the estate so as to seek out his lady love. They were busy days. The large staff had been presented to the new mistress of Whisperwood and she was beginning to know them and to like the smiling faces that reflected both fondness for the master and approval of his lady. At Cliveden's urging Mrs. Vernon now devoted all her time to her beloved Mrs. Hammond. The bride interviewed several well-qualified candidates of whom she was sure she would be terrified, and next saw a very thin and nervous country girl who was obviously desperately eager to become her personal maid. Emma Camden's experience was limited, but her single reference was impressive, and she had a soft voice and gentle manner. Helena's kind heart was touched when she learned that the girl was all alone in the world and had used her last sixpence to bribe a carter to bring her to Whisperwood. Emma fainted dead away when she was hired, and from that day on served her young mistress with such devotion that Helena never had occasion to regret her choice.

Cliveden conducted Helena about the village and surrounding countryside, and neighbours began to pay bride calls. The vicar and his wife were among those visiting and the lady, being a great animal lover, struck up an immediate friendship with Mrs. Hammond. Emmett explored happily with his puppy, Wagger, frolicking along beside him; rode or fished with Cliveden; or strolled into the village. He was very soon involved in a brawl and came home with a black eye and the glad tidings that he'd met two "jolly good fellows."

The bedchamber remodelling progressed with smooth efficiency. The offending chimneypiece was removed, and with the intent of commissioning a suitable replacement, Cliveden drove Helena to the establishment of a renowned stonemason in Tunbridge Wells. Her bright eyes lit upon a fine old chimneypiece which had been taken from a great house ruined by fire and lay all but forgotten in a corner of the stonemason's shed. It was covered with dust and cobwebs, but when the apprentices cleaned the surface, it was found to depict nymphs bathing in a woodland glade, the central scene set within a frieze rich with birds and flowers. The workmanship was exquisite, and Cliveden was as pleased with the piece as was his bride. The stonemason said that he must come to Whisperwood to take exact measurements, but that if the information Cliveden had brought was reasonably accurate, there would be few adjustments required and he should be able to complete the installation in short order. When he quoted the price, Helena gave a gasp, but Cliveden seemed undismayed and they left, mutually pleased with their purchase.

The weather had improved at last, and it was a brilliant day with only a few fluffy white clouds drifting about an azure sky. Cliveden had driven his curricle and the open air brought a glow to Helena's cheeks while the sight of numerous fashionable vehicles and carefree little groups of shoppers lightened her spirits. By contrast, her husband became quiet and rather grim.

"Oh, look, Cliveden," she exclaimed eagerly. "It is the Pantiles Arcade. They say it is very nice and I should so like to see it. May we stop?"

"By all means," he said, turning the team onto a side street. "Another day, perhaps. I've a parcel to collect at the other end of town, and to say truth, m'dear, I'm a trifle tired."

She hid her disappointment, and although she looked rather wistfully at the busy streets, made no further request to delay. Cliveden stopped at a cottage on the outskirts of the town, and she held the reins while he went inside, to return almost at once carrying a long, unwieldy parcel. It seemed to her critical gaze that he was walking quite well without his cane. Better, in fact, than since he had come home from Spain. Further, he did not look at all tired, and having slid his burden under the seats, mounted the curricle with an easy swing.

He slanted an oblique glance at her and said with his quirkish half-smile, "I think you are displeased. My regrets, madam wife. I will try to mend my fences by taking you to a pleasant inn for luncheon."

He took the Hastings Road, and Helena supposed he knew of some "pleasant inn" situated on the outskirts of town, but he drove for some miles before turning into the ill-kept yard of a rather run down old tavern. Helena thought it lonely and uninviting, and the food was no better than average. Cliveden kept up a steady stream of conversation, and Helena was polite but she could not help but be irritated when she recalled the many charming hostelries in the Wells where they might have lunched more agreeably.

As if divining her thoughts, he murmured, "I grant you that this is not an extreme elegant spot, Mrs. Cliveden. But it has attractions that are perhaps not readily apparent."

She wondered if he referred to the host's pretty but pert little spouse, who had fluttered her lashes at him so boldly when they arrived. She asked with a teasing smile, "Attractions having red hair, sir?"

"Decidedly not." He grinned as she watched him, mystified, and finished, "There is not a cat in sight! At least, not of the four-legged variety."

She laughed merrily. "I expect I deserved that setdown. Poor Cliveden. We have properly disrupted your quiet existence."

"I have few complaints. One being that I have another name, you know."

She gave him a startled look and he said wryly, "I had hoped we might be friends Helena, if nothing more."

"Good gracious, I think we are far from enemies, sir—ah, Peter." The name sounded strange on her tongue, and she blushed and for some ridiculous reason felt shy. "How could I be anything but grateful?"

He raised one hand in a dismissive gesture. "No, please. I don't want your gratitude. I would rather think you had come to like me a little."

"Indeed, I have never disliked you."

"Have you not?" Reaching across the table, he took up her hand. "Yet sometimes I see unhappiness in your eyes. I don't want you to be unhappy, m'dear. Is it only because you love another man?"

The abruptness of the question took her breath away. She looked down and said quietly, "Alas, I fear we both know that sorrow."

He stared at her, then shrugged. "Oh no. I by far prefer the ladies."

Her gaze shot back to him. Again, he showed a solemn mouth even as his eyes danced with laughter. She tried to be stern, but could not keep back a giggle. On the return drive to Whisperwood she entered willingly into a discussion of his plans to fully restore the original house located about a quarter mile behind the present structure.

He said earnestly, "It is part of England's heritage, you know. William the Conqueror was here, and Simon de Montfort—who fought for our right to a parliament—and Roundheads and Royalists—" He saw her watching him with amusement, and broke off, flushing. "Egad, how wordy I become. Your pardon, ma'am, I—Jove, but I've done it again! Now how do I offend?"

She tossed her curls. "If you object to the word 'sir,' then I may object to 'ma'am,' which is far more odious."

"Odious is it? Why?"

"Because..." a dimple peeped at him, "I am your wife, not a mere acquaintance."

Cliveden gazed at her and a tenderness crept into his eyes seeming to hypnotize her so that she could neither turn away nor had the least wish to do so. The team slowed, unnoticed, until the curricle rocked to the thundering passage of a stagecoach that all but forced them into the ditch. The driver guffawed while his passengers stared, grinning, from the windows.

The guard on the coach shouted, "Silly moonling! Marry the wench and do your fondling at home!"

Cliveden set his jaw. "Hang on tight, my love." He sent his whip cracking over the horses' heads and they sprang into a gallop. The road was very narrow. Helena gasped and clung to the side, praying that her husband knew what he was about. Glancing at him she was surprised to see him leaning forward slightly, a faint smile curving his mouth, his eyes sparkling. His hands on the reins were skilled and sure. The curricle raced past the lumbering stagecoach, and left the guard and driver swearing in a cloud of dust as it shot out before them.

"Peter," laughed Helena, her heart thundering. "I think Emmett would say you drive to an inch! I wonder I am not fallen down in a swoon."

"Thank you. But actually, I belive we cleared their wheels by about two inches, so there was no cause for alarm. And you've your share of pluck, my Helena. Not a squeak out of you, far less a swoon!"

She felt inordinately pleased. "I have three madcap brothers you know, and am used to the pranks of foolish boys."

"I hope you do not so classify me, ma'am." He twinkled at her. "In some quarters I am held to be a very dull dog."

Eastleigh had said that of him. She wondered how well Robert had known her husband, and what he would have thought if he'd seen that splendid piece of driving. Her high spirits sank, and she realized with a pang of guilt that her lost love had been far from her mind for some days now....

A gloved hand closed over her wrist. Cliveden said in a contrite voice, "No, did I really scare you, m'dear? I make you my apologies."

He was peering at her anxiously. She felt traitorous and gabbled that she'd been not in the least scared, then, in an attempt to change the subject, asked what he meant to do with the old house after it was restored.

"I thought it would be nice as a sort of Dower House for your mama and your brothers. They could be close, yet we could be more—er, private." He had spoken almost carelessly, but from under his lashes he watched her intently. "Does the notion appeal to you?"

A tiny frown puckered her brow, and she folded her hands in the way she had when she was deep in thought. "I think," she answered, choosing her words with care, "that question has many ramifications—Mr. Cliveden."

He chuckled. "And I am thrown in the close—as usual. And reduced to Mr. Cliveden again. I stand corrected—ma'am."

Helena eyed him gravely. "Do you know, sir, if ours was not a *mariage de convenance*, I might almost think you were flirting."

"But since ours *is* a *mariage de convenance*, that would not be likely. Would it, my Helena?"

"Not at all likely. Peter." But was it her imagination, or did his voice hold just the hint of a caress whenever he said "My Helena"? She smiled to herself. At all events, it was rather nice.

When they reached the house, Rostyn's chair was on the terrace. He looked pale and irritated and said with an ominous spark in his dark eyes that he hoped they'd enjoyed their day more than he'd enjoyed his.

Cliveden waved away the footman and handed Helena down himself. She hurried to her brother and said lovingly, "We found a fine new chimneypiece, dearest. What have you been about to make you so cross?"

Glaring at his brother-in-law who was retrieving his parcel from under the seat, Rostyn waited until a lackey drove the curricle away, then said, "I'll thank your husband to refrain from offering my skills to everyone in creation."

"Feel incompetent, do you?" drawled Cliveden.

"Damme but I don't!"

"Then I fail to see why you'd object."

"As I told you before, I know nothing of veterinary medicine!"

Bewildered, Helena said, "Ross, what on earth are you talking about?"

Cliveden sighed. "I'd thought Hammond wanted to be useful, so—"

"So he has spread the word I am an amateur veterinary," snarled Rostyn. "And I've been damned near inundated by a constant stream of people bringing me everything from a sick canary to a blasted great Welsh bull!"

Helena threw a concealing hand over her smile.

"Well then," said Cliveden reasonably, "it proves there's a need, my dear fellow and you *can* be of use, after all. If you only apply yourself."

Rostyn's nostrils flared with rage. "I'll be of .lamned *small* use to *you*, by God! None of these folks can pay—even had I the gall to charge 'em for doing what little I can, so never think I can give you my ill-gotten gains."

Appalled, Helena saw Cliveden's brows pull down sharply. "But you do have a way with animals, Ross," she interjected. "You always have. Only look at how the puppy's nose is healing so well."

"Oh, pshaw!" snorted her brother, and pulled impatiently at the wheels of his chair.

Cliveden stopped his retreat by the simple expedient of sticking the narrow end of his parcel between the spokes of one wheel. "If you are determined to make me support a perpetual invalid, Hammond, you likely won't have the least wish to try these, either." He tore the wrapping from his parcel and dumped two crutches across the arms of the chair.

Helena gave a shocked cry, but her instinctive defence of her brother was cut off. His face livid, Rostyn grabbed one crutch and flailed it upward.

"Peter!" shrieked Helena.

Cliveden stood very still, watching the invalid unwaveringly.

His face contorted with rage, Rostyn checked, then hurled the crutch away and half-sobbed, *"Damn you,* Cliveden! You may have bought my sister, but you've not bought *me!* By God, when I get out of this chair, you'd best—" And with an inarticulate gulp he wheeled back into the house.

Horrified, Helena started after him.

Cliveden caught her arm. "Let him go. Perhaps anger will stir his blood if nothing else can."

She turned on him furiously. "Oh, how *could* you! Why must you add to his misery by taunting him all the time? Have you no compassion? No understanding of what he's going through?"

"Of course I understand what he's going through. I merely wonder for how long he means to enjoy it!"

"Enjoy!" she exclaimed, bristling. "Of all the arrogant—"

"Nonsense! A man has to exert himself if he's to—" He broke off with an irked cry as Wagger raced from the house and tore past, growling fiercely, and shaking the prize gripped between his jaws. "My new slippers!" roared Cliveden and made an futile grab for the miscreant. Threats, lunges, and commands failed. Ears flapping, the puppy gamboled and crouched and bounced around the enraged man and then rushed off into the garden.

"Blasted brute," panted Cliveden, limping back to his wife and glowering at her hilarity.

"Did you successfully *exert* yourself, dear?" she gasped tearfully.

He stared at her laughing face and the anger in his own faded. "Wretched spouse!" He seized her wrist and swung her to him, smiling down at her. His hands slipped to her shoulders.

Helena's mirth was replaced by unease. Looking around nervously she saw a mob-capped head dart from sight at an upper window. "The—the servants," she stammered. "They're watching us."

"Let 'em." His long fingers cradled her cheek. "We *are* supposed to be newlyweds, you know. How very smooth your skin is.... I really think you might *try* to pretend you find me irresistible, my love."

"Is that what *you* are doing?" she asked, wondering why she allowed herself to sway to him a little. "Pretending?"

"I have no need to pretend...."

His voice was very soft, and the caress in it was echoed in his eyes. Shocked, and frightened because she was at once trembling and oddly elated, Helena gazed up at him speechlessly.

His lips quirked. "Because," he went on, "I *know* I am irresistible." But even as she chuckled, relieved by his whimsicality, he threw her offstride once more. "And the man who had to *pretend* to find you so must be a proper noddycock. You are a very beautiful girl, my Helena."

"I am no longer a girl," she said faintly, noting as if for the first time how well-shaped were his lips. "I am a wife."

He bent above her and murmured, "Ah, but—in name only...."

This conversation was not going at all properly. Helena, in fact, had the sensation that she was being dragged into an inescapable whirlpool. Panicking, she pulled away from him. "It was what we agreed upon, Mr. Cliveden. But our bargain did not give you the right to maul me."

He stiffened and said with a satiric bow, "My apologies."

Helena fled.

Alone in her parlour, except for Soot, Delilah and Windy Wallets, all of whom had followed her upstairs and now insisted upon admittance, she sat in the windowseat, prey to a very uneasy conscience. Cliveden was rather merciless with poor Ross, but otherwise he'd been so good, and more than lived up to his bargain. Until now. But he was only a man, and men were so... She looked apprehensively at the closed connecting door to her husband's bedchamber, and shivered. As if sensing that she was upset, Windy Wallets jumped onto her lap. She was glad of the sympathy, and began to explain matters. This was a mistake, because Windy Wallets could seldom be relied upon for a simple answer, but tended to reduce any conversation to a monologue. He did so now, voicing his opinions with such raucous vehemence that she at last told him he was a typical overbearing male, and went off in search of human companionship.

In the hall a lackey bowed and responded to her question by advising that Master Emmett and his friends were in the weapons room where the master was instructing them in the art of fence. Mildly surprised, Helena thanked him, and chancing to encounter the steward leaving the study, exchanged a few words with that gentleman, then asked, "Have you been with my husband for a long while, Mr. Shafer?"

"In a manner of speaking, Mrs. Cliveden. I served the General till Sir Ian and his lady went out to India. A fine gentleman he is, too, but never liked Whisperwood, which is why he made it over to Mr. Peter, I suppose. And the *old* gentleman—Sir Ian's father—a bit of a tartar *he* was! A far cry from Mr. Peter, who never shouts, nor throws things at the servants, but gets his way just the same—if I may remark on it."

'Good gracious,' thought Helena. "I believe Mr. Cliveden is interested in fencing, no?"

"Yes indeed, ma'am. Quite a master he used to be. Pity he can't enjoy a bout with the foils no more, but you'll never hear him complain, for he ain't that sort. A regular plucked 'un he is, and—Now only listen to me telling you something you already know, as if you wasn't the master's wife!"

Helena smiled and left him, wondering why Cliveden won such devotion from his people, and hearing him say teasingly, "Ah—but in name only...."

She was roused by the sound of Rostyn's anger, and having knocked at his door and gone unheard, went inside. Her mother was trying to calm him, but he was in a proper rage. Catching sight of Helena, he shouted, "It's as well, Mrs. Cliveden, that yours is no more than a *mariage de convenance*, for when I am well again, I've every intent to knock down your arrogant boor of a husband. At the very least!"

A sudden and unfamiliar fury possessed Helena. Drawing herself up, she said, haughtily, "Why? For having been nothing but good to us all? For trying to rouse you from wallowing in self-pity? Or is it because you are so mean-spirited as to refuse to admit you need his protection, if only temporarily?" And she turned on her heel and left him staring after her with his eyes stricken and his mouth hanging open.

SAVE FOR THE MUFFLED UPROAR emanating from Cliveden's bedchamber, the rest of the week passed peacefully enough. Helena and Mrs. Hammond were invited to tea at the Vicarage; the squire and his lady paid a morning call. Sir Walter Wansford, whose lands marched with Whisperwood on the east, drove over with an elderly and beloved spaniel which had run a thorn into its pad. Rostyn, who had emerged from his room to go to the library, was unable to hide in time. He succeeded in removing the thorn much to Sir Walter's delight, and then beat a hasty retreat.

The baronet returned next day with his wife, who was clearly charmed by the bride. A note was delivered that afternoon asking that the newlyweds join a small party which would journey to Town next week to dine, attend the theatre, then overnight at the Wansford's Berkeley Street house. The thought of a jolly group and a trip to the metropolis brought stars into Helena's eyes, and she began to plan her wardrobe, but her joy was premature. Cliveden had another engagement he was "quite unable to break." He apologized for her disappointment and told her he would take her to the theatre himself, but when she pressed him for a date, he said vaguely that he'd have to look at his appointment calendar, as there was much to be done about the estate before the heat of the summer.

She was changing her dress that afternoon when her abigail brought a note from the master. He regretted that he was called away "on a matter of urgent business" and would probably not return in time for dinner. It was as much as Helena could do to conceal her vexation. Tonight they were to entertain the local *grande dame*, her simpering daughter and her vacuous son. Helena had only met the family once, but it had been sufficient to make her dread the evening. There would be an odd number at table, since Mrs. Hammond was invited to dine at the Vicarage, and to add insult to injury, Helena must receive guests she scarce knew, with only Emmett to play host, for Rostyn had avoided her since their quarrel and no longer joined the family for dinner.

When she discreetly questioned Mr. Shafer as to the master's "urgent business," the steward replied with such bland evasions that she was suddenly shocked into the realization that she challenged forbidden territory: her husband had at last decided to visit his inamorata.

It was like a dash of cold water in her face. She felt stunned and betrayed, and enumerating her grievances decided that it was bitterly unfair. He had spoiled their day in Tunbridge Wells; refused her a

delightful trip to London; and now was so unprincipled as to abandon her to this trio of colossal bores
while he slithered off to spend the night with his paramour! The man was not only a libertine, but he was
anti-social besides!

When she went downstairs however, she was overjoyed to find the invalid chair already awaiting her in
the lower hall. Very handsome in evening dress, her
elder brother regarded her with a contrite smile. "I'm
sorry, little sister. Will you forgive? You are perfectly
right and I'm an ungrateful clod."

She kissed him, and assured him that there was
nothing to forgive.

"Not yet," he said, lowering his voice as Emmett
hurried to join them. "But I still mean to knock
Cliveden down, blast his ears!"

"Good," said Helena.

"I WOULD NOT DISTURB your concentration, my
dear," murmured Cliveden, watching Helena select
and cut a delicate pink peony, "but I wondered
whether you might speak to me today. I should like to
be prepared with some dazzling rejoinder, you see."

She turned to him, her eyes very wide over the great
bloom she held to her pretty nose, and said innocently, "I was not aware I had stopped speaking to
you, Mr. Cliveden."

He flinched and pressed one slim hand to his brow.
"Mr. Cliveden! Gad!"

He looked so grieved that Helena had to fight a
smile, the resultant dimples bringing such a glow to her
husband's eyes that she blushed.

"You have not spoken to me since your dinner party," he said with a great sigh.

Indignant, she retorted, "I most certainly have! I wished you good morning yesterday when you at length came home, and—"

"And good afternoon, and good evening, and you did not speak *to* me, ma'am, but *at* me. A vast difference." Here, her eyes chancing to meet his, he smiled and stepped closer, saying softly, "My poor wife. Was the dinner party so very dreadful?"

He was not an *exceeding* handsome man, yet when that particular smile lit the grey eyes, it was difficult to resist his charm. And he had, after all, a perfect right to see his lady love. (Who was probably all bosom and giggle and well past her prime.) "Perfectly dreadful," replied Helena, trying to look stern. "Had Rostyn not kindly come to my rescue you'd likely have returned home to find me laid down on my bed in an expiring condition!"

He pursed his lips. "Oh, no."

She watched him uncertainly.

"Your fierce new abigail would never admit me," he finished blandly. "I believe she thinks I—er, have no right in your bed. I mean—bedchamber."

Helena's eyes fell and her blush deepened. "Emma has no reason to suppose—I mean, our agreement is not common knowledge."

"Certainly not!" He said musingly, "I wonder if that is why I keep forgetting about it."

"Do you so?" Recovering some vestiges of common sense she retaliated, "I had thought you had it well in mind when you evaded our dinner party, sir."

For a moment he was silent, then he bent and with his pocket knife cut a glowing red blossom. "Touché," he drawled, presenting the peony to her with a graceful bow. Diverted, she did not at once notice that in the process, he had somehow moved much nearer. Before she could draw back, his hand was caressing her cheek. "But, do you know, my Helena," he said, his voice very soft, "I really think I dislike 'sir' even more than 'Mr. Cliveden.'"

His fingers were warm and gentle yet made her skin tingle in a most disquieting way. He was very close now, looking down at her with a wistful tenderness that suspended her ability to breathe.

"It is not . . . fair . . ." she managed feebly.

He ran one fingertip around her lips. "I am glad you admit it."

"*Admit . . . ?*" she gasped.

"Yes. For—be honest—you make no least attempt to cooperate." He pressed a kiss into her trembling little palm. "But persist in being. . ." He bent lower. "Much too beautiful." The flame that came into his eyes melted away her resistance. "I do try," he murmured, drawing her into his arms, "but—" She lifted her face, her eyes closing. . . .

"I shall ask you, sir," bellowed a harsh, loud voice, "how *dare* you behave in so disgraceful a manner?"

"*Confound* it all!" said Cliveden through his teeth.

Helena's eyes flew open. Jerking away, her face scarlet, she saw an even redder face: large, jowly, and uncompromisingly aggressive. Hot with embarrassment, she waited for her husband to forcibly eject this impertinent person.

"I put it to you, sir," drawled Cliveden, straightening the neckcloth to which Helena had been clinging, and turning to face his large and irate visitor, "that this is my home, and this lady is my wife."

"So I should hope, sir! Indeed! That does not mitigate your offense!"

"Offense!" exclaimed Helena, indignant.

"A most dastardly offense, madam!"

"What I do on my own lands—" began Cliveden reasonably.

Helena could not but think of what Robert Eastleigh would have done by this time. Cliveden, of course, was still recuperating from wounds, and tall as he was, this horrible gentleman—for there could be no doubt he was a gentleman—fairly towered over him.

"You've no right to steal another man's property," roared the interloper. Helena felt very cold, and dared not look at her husband. If this was some friend of dear Robert's, Cliveden would have a perfect right to call him out for such a remark. She waited breathlessly for a deadly challenge.

Cliveden frowned. "I believe I have not your acquaintance, Mr....?"

"You'd not have it now, by God, save that I've had to track you down and follow you all the way from Town. I am Page-Welwyn, sir. And you are a rascal and a villain! Wrapped up the business quickly and ran here to hide, did you not? By Jove, but I've a mind to black your eye for you!"

He really was very large and looked as flushed and murderous as Cliveden was calm. 'If he strikes Peter,' thought Helena, 'there will be a duel.'

"You quite terrify me, Mr. Page-Welwyn," drawled Cliveden mildly. "Would you care to be a shade more explicit?"

Helena stepped closer to her husband, dreading what was to come.

It came in the form of an ear-splitting yowl, and being the farthest thing from her mind caused Helena to give an involuntary jump into the air, which was fortunate as she barely missed the large and well equipped paw that flashed out in retaliation. The ugliest of their cats sat down and eyed her with resentment. "Oh, my poor one," she said, gathering up the animal and stroking him fondly. "Did I tread on your toe?"

"God, if that don't beat the Dutch!" exclaimed Page-Welwyn. "Have you no shame, madam?"

Belatedly, it dawned on Helena that they entertained a madman.

"No, I really cannot permit that you take that tone to my wife, Mr. Page-Welwyn." The cat was wriggling, and Cliveden removed it from Helena's arms. "Let me have Windy Wallets, m'dear, and you go and—"

"Windy Wallets?" roared the intruder. "Take your hands off that animal!"

"Now see here," remonstrated Cliveden, glancing at Helena and jerking his head towards the house. "He may be an ugly brute, but—"

"You, sir," roared the big man, "are a fool, sir, not to wrap it up in clean linen! I am come after Faro!"

Backing away, Helena thought, 'Good heavens!' and went quickly towards the house in search of men to restrain the lunatic.

"Er—are you indeed," said Cliveden, keeping a wary eye on this strange individual. "Regrettably, I am an indifferent card player, so—"

"With a 'p' and an 'h', sir!" howled Page-Welwyn.

Frowning, Cliveden began to see the light. "Pharoah...? Do you say that our poor old Windy Wallets is—"

"Is my property, you cat-napping scoundrel! A most rare and valuable Egyptian cat, sir, as if you didn't know it! My poor wife's heart is quite broke! I've had to advertise and search and traipse all this way to rescue the dear little chap, and you add insult to injury by naming him—By God, but I'll have your blood for that alone!" Purple with wrath, he advanced.

"No," sighed Cliveden, putting down the cat, "do you really think—"

He had no opportunity to finish his remark.

ENCOUNTERING EMMETT on the terrace steps, Helena sent him running to try and prevent his brother-in-law's murder. She hurried into the house and gathered three sturdy footmen whom she also despatched post haste to the rescue of their employer, and followed them, her heart pounding with dread. She had reached the terrace when Emmett raced across the lawn shouting for towels—"Quick!" With a gasp of terror, she flew back inside, returning to thrust some linens into her brother's ready hands.

"Emmett—is Cliveden—"

"If ever I saw...so much blood," he panted, and sprinted off again towards the distant cutting gardens.

Helena stood as one turned to stone. The verdant scene blurred before her eyes, and she was suddenly very cold. If he should die...

As from a great distance she saw one of the footmen run up the drivepath calling for a carriage. Were they going for a surgeon? She forced her trembling limbs to carry her down the steps and began to hurry across the lawn. Emmett came running to her. He was breathless and... *laughing!*

"Oh, Helena," he gasped. "What a nonsensical thing! Poor Cliveden pays a price for having wed us, by Jove, but he does!"

She seized him by his neckcloth, and clung to it. "Is he hurt?"

"Let be!" He removed her clutch, grumbling, "Why you women must always ruin a man's garments when you go up in the boughs is beyond me." Her white little face put a stop to his words. He said, "No cause for your Drury Lane airs, Nell. Jove, but to look at you, one would think there'd been murder done, and it's nothing worse than that poor Cliveden was obliged to draw that great block's cork. Your husband, m'dear, has the fastest right I ever saw!"

Overwhelmed with relief, she gasped. "P-Peter...actually *struck* Mr. Page-Welwyn? But—but you said he p-paid a price, and so I thought—"

"Well so he does, poor fellow," he said, chuckling. "What with Rostyn behaving like the melancholy

Dane, and having me to support, and Mama foisting
all her silly cats on him, and now this wild man coming to knock him down. To say nothing of you playing off your touch-me-not airs, when—"

"He was m-mad, of course," she intervened hurriedly.

"Page-Welwyn? Oh, as fire! And," he laughed,
"*how* his nose bleeds! And to think poor Cliveden
thought he wanted to play—c-cards...!"

"But—he did. He said he came for faro. I heard
him!"

"Pharoah, love. The Egyptian. It appears that's
Windy Wallet's real name, and the fellow accused
Cliveden of cat-napping the ugly brute."

Helena clasped her hands and peered up at him.
"Oh, no! And—and do you say Peter really knocked
him down? But—he was so very big! And Cliveden is
so—I mean, he's such a timid soul."

Emmett gave another whoop. "I wouldn't refine on
that too much m'dear," he chortled. "No, really I
wouldn't."

CHAPTER SIX

"BUT MAMA," PROTESTED HELENA, adjusting the orange grosgrain ribbon that threaded her shining curls, "We shall be late as it is, and I promised Lady Wansford I would help at the needlework booth."

"Yes, my love." Prettily petite in a dark red velvet tunic over a white satin gown trimmed with gold, Mrs. Hammond tugged at her daughter's arm. "But the Fete has probably not even begun, and everything is always a muddle for the first hour or two. Was you thinking of wearing this?" She lifted First Cat from the transparent stole that lay on the bed. "Oh dear, it is a little bent. Do hurry, sweet child. I vow I was never more delighted!"

Helena allowed the "bent" stole to be draped about her shoulders and accompanied her mother to the stairs. Her request to know what was so delightful was interrupted by a faint scream. "Your slippers are *white*!" cried Mrs. Hammond. "You forgot the orange sherbet ones you had made to match that delicious gown. You must go and change! Oh, what a botheration!"

"I cannot, Mama, for I have lost one. Wagger must have taken it."

"That naughty puppy." Mrs. Hammond proceeded down the stairs. "He is unnerving all the cats,
you know, and yesterday I saw him eating something
that looked very much like the pen from Cliveden's
Standish.

Helena smiled. "Poor Cliveden. Alas, I fear Emmett was right when he said my husband paid a high
price to wed me."

"Fiddlesticks! He was generous, I'll allow, but
would have paid ten times the amount to win you. And
rightly so, for where else could he have found so lovely
a wife, who is such a credit to him?"

It was the second time a member of her family had
implied her husband had married from more than a
sense of obligation, and Helena felt her cheeks grow
hot. The outer air did little to cool them, for although
it was only eleven o'clock, the day was very warm.
Mrs. Hammond set a brisk pace, and accompanied by
Turnip and Warrior (who ventured forth bravely despite his fear of magpies), they made their way into the
pleasant shade of the woods and thence to the old
ruins that Cliveden intended to transform to the
Dower House.

"Mama," Helena protested, somewhat out of
breath. "What on earth—"

"Sshhh!" Mrs. Hammond tiptoed across the stretch
of turf to the side of the house and the vast chamber
that had once been a music room. She gestured urgently. "Only look, my love," she whispered. "Is it
not marvellous?"

Cupping her hands about her eyes, Helena peered
through a broken pane of the mullioned window. It

was indeed marvellous. With Daniels walking close beside him, Rostyn was struggling along on the despised crutches Cliveden had brought him. Even as two loving pairs of eyes watched, one of the crutches slipped, and Rostyn tumbled. The ladies gave joint gasps and clutched one another in terror, but Daniel's arms had already whipped about the invalid.

"Wonderful, sir!" exclaimed the tall man. "You went the whole length today. Oh, how proud the master would be to see it!"

"Proud?" panted Rostyn, short of breath and sagging wearily. "He fancies me a whining failure! But I'll . . . show him, blast his eyes!"

"Of course you will," agreed Daniels stoutly. "And then you'll knock him down for his arrogance, eh, sir?"

"You may believe I will, Mr. Impertinence!"

"Well, in the meantime, Mr. Hammond, you've clients waiting."

"Devil take it," groaned Rostyn. "What that hound has wished upon me!"

"Shall I tell them you cannot see them, sir?"

"Yes, yes! I'm of no mind to bother with the silly idiots. Wheel me back to the house, there's a good fellow."

Daniels assisted Rostyn into the invalid chair, and the two tearful spies began to creep away, but paused when they heard Rostyn ask nonchalantly who was waiting.

"No one to matter, sir," answered Daniels with equal nonchalance. "A little village lad weeping over his mongrel who was caught in a trap."

Rostyn said hotly, "What the deuce d'you mean—
'no one to matter'? I'll wager it would matter was it
your own animal. Poor little devil! How long has he
been waiting? Take me in there at once, you villain!"
The irate voice faded, and Mrs. Hammond sniffed
unashamedly, and dabbed at her eyes with the tiny
wisp of cambric and lace that served her as a handkerchief. Helena was no less affected, and it was a
moment before she was able to command her voice.
"Oh, Mama, how wonderful! And how very good
Daniels is with him, and manages him just as slyly as,
ah—"

"As our dear Cliveden," put in Mrs. Hammond,
taking up Warrior, who had become stiff upon sight-
ing a magpie. "I have been thinking, you know," she
went on, as they turned back towards the main house,
"that you might wish to name your firstborn after
Papa. Now he is quite gone away, Warrior, so you may
stop your shivering. Had you not such pretty silver fur
they might not always be trying to steal it for their
nests. And George is a good name for any man. But
Peter is a fine name also."

Her face burning, Helena said, "We must make
haste, Mama, or they will catch up with us and I'd not
spoil Rostyn's surprise for the world."

"They will not follow, and that is another surprise," said Mrs. Hammond. "Daniels has made a
room of the old house into a sort of dispensary for
your brother. I peeped in and truly it looks so profes-
sional! Emmett told me that Rostyn studies every day
while he tells us he is sleeping, and people are starting
to come to his little clinic."

"Good gracious! Has he a real interest, do you think?"

"I do indeed. And I believe your husband somehow discovered it, so has conspired with Daniels to achieve all this."

The surge of gratitude Helena felt was followed by a most disquieting thought. The stonemason had finished his work, and the new carpets were being laid today. There remained only the selection and purchasing of new furniture. She had, in fact, asked Peter to drive her into Town so that they might visit some warehouses, but he'd said they would do just as well in Dorking, which was so much more convenient. After that, the master bedchamber would be finished.... He would occupy it—so close to her! A little tremor of delicious fright crept between her shoulder blades.

"Thank goodness, here is the carriage," exclaimed Mrs. Hammond. "And as well, my love. Only look how the heat has made you colour up!"

"Yes, Mama," said Helena meekly.

It was even warmer (but Helena was less flushed) when they reached Wansford Lodge. The lawns all around the square grey mansion were a mass of brightly coloured tents, booths, and stands, gay with flags and bunting, where a jostling, noisily happy crowd vied and bartered for the used clothing, china and glassware, cooking implements, art works, fine needlepoint, dainty reticules, patchwork quilts, eiderdowns, hand-knitted scarves, gloves and caps, and numerous other useful items, all donated for the benefit of maimed soldiers returning from the war. As is usually the case at such gatherings, humanity's concern for self-gratification was paramount, and the food stands were lost from sight amid the mob surrounding them.

Mrs. Hammond was swept up by a group of friends when they left their carriage, and Helena made her way to the needlework booth. She was heartily welcomed by Miss Murray, a thin and shy little spinster, who was striving to cope with this unexpectedly large crowd. Helena scarcely had time to put off her gloves than she fell victim to a large young woman wearing a startlingly low-cut gown who demanded the price of practically every item on display and then declared them all too dear and flaunted away, remarking that she would have a pork pie instead. Fortunately, Helena's other customers were far easier to please, and the hours flew past. She was beginning to be tired and thirsty when a gentleman's voice drawled,

"She surely was the fairest there
Of all the fairs at the country fair!"

Startled, she looked up and met a pair of pale blue eyes that at the moment reflected a wistful admiration.

"Mr. Savage!" she exclaimed, reaching out to him joyously.

He took her hands, his eyes lighting up. "I am forgiven! What a generous heart you possess, dear lady! Ah, if you but knew how I have regretted my gauche behaviour. I offer a thousand apologies for it."

Helena had been so pleased to see an old friend that she had quite forgotten the manner of their parting. Blushing, she tried to draw her hands away, but before relinquishing them, Savage pressed each in turn to his lips. "There is nothing for it," he declared. "Against my better nature, I rather like your husband. It is rare that I entertain such kindly feelings. Still, I must sacrifice him. I shall call him out and put a period to him, and thus clear my path to the prize I so stupidly allowed to escape me!"

"Goodness me," fluttered Miss Murray, staring in horror at this elegant but murderously inclined young man.

Laughingly exasperated, Helena presented Savage and begged that the timid lady pay him no heed. "He pretends to be very naughty, but I assure you, Miss Murray, it is all fustian."

"I see you have correctly read my brother's character," cried Geraldine, coming up to embrace Helena. "Oh, how well you look in that lovely orange gown! Marriage becomes you, my dear."

"And would become her far better did her last name commence with an 'S' rather than a 'C'," put in Savage.

"Only see how desirable I am, now that I am safely wed," teased Helena. "Come, sir. If you mean to loiter here, you must buy something."

"By all means." Leopold turned to bow to Miss Murray. "I shall take that lace-trimmed gown. I am sure my sister would look well in it."

Miss Murray squealed with amusement. "Not unless she is in the habit of wearing curtains, sir!" His

wink turned her gaunt cheeks a bright pink, and she
flirted happily with him while he showed a marked and
quite insincere interest in the items she recommended.

Geraldine said, "How I have missed you, dearest
Nell. I've *so* much to tell you! How is Mr. Hammond? Oh, just look at all the people coming this
way! If only we could talk somewhere."

"So we shall, I promise. My brother is much better, thank heaven! You must come and see him. Are
you established in the country for long?"

"Forever, if necessary," smiled Leopold, turning to
them. "May I bring my sister to call on you tomorrow, ma'am? I've a wager placed on a London-to-
Brighton curricle race, and they'll be changing teams
near Whisperwood so I'll be in your vicinity. And I
have earned a treat, have I not, Miss Murray?"

"You have indeed," trilled his unwitting foil. "Only
think, Mrs. Cliveden, the kind gentleman has bought
everything! *Everything!* And donated it all back to us
again. Such generosity!"

"In which case I can deny him nothing," said Helena, adding, as she saw the gleam in his eyes, "within
reason. I shall look forward to your company for dinner tomorrow, Mr. Savage. Do try to arrive early
Gerry, so that we can have a nice cose. Rostyn will be
so glad when I tell him you are coming."

As Mrs. Hammond had accepted an invitation to
dine at the Lodge, it was almost midnight before they
returned home. Helena was rather disappointed that
Cliveden had not waited up for her, as he usually did
on the rare occasions when she went out without him.
Her disappointment turned to pique when Emma gave

her a note in which her husband advised that he had been obliged to drive into Town, but would return before noon the following day. She was tired, but when the bedcurtains were drawn and the drowsy abigail had blown out the candles and sought her own bed, Helena did not sink into sleep, but lay frowning at the peculiarly shaped lump in the canopy that normally billowed above her.

Cliveden had refused to attend the garden fete, claiming he had much business to transact with Mr. Shafer. But Emma had remarked in all innocence that within ten minutes of madam's departure the master had ordered his bag packed and a team harnessed to the high-perch phaeton. Cliveden was considerate of those who served him; he certainly would not have left had he expected the steward. He must have already made plans to go into London. Knowing how much she longed to visit the metropolis, he had denied her the opportunity to accompany him. She could very easily have asked Verny to take her place at the garden fete. But perhaps her company would have been unwelcome; perhaps, even at this moment his peculiar lay in his arms!

Helena sat bolt upright in bed. "Oh!" she exclaimed, suddenly tearful. "How horridly sly!" The lump in the upper drapery burst into frantic activity. A brown-and-white face peered through the top of the bedcurtains, and in another second, Delilah had leapt onto the bed and was doing her feline best to comfort her afflicted human.

ROSTYN WAS JUST AS PLEASED to welcome their guests as Helena had supposed he would be. She hid her own feelings of ill usage, and knew she had no least right to resent an arrangement to which she had willingly agreed. Only, Cliveden had not abided by the rules either; flirting with her quite outrageously but then forgetting all about her and slinking off to his revolting paramour in so underhanded a way.

Their guests arrived at three o'clock in a gleaming phaeton of rich chocolate brown. Cliveden had still not returned, nor had Rostyn made an appearance, and only Mrs. Hammond, Emmett, and Helena greeted their friends. Geraldine looked a little slimmer and was remarkably pretty in a pale lemon gown with embroidered golden dots on the ruffle and repeated on the shawl draped across her elbows. Nothing would do but that Helena must show them about the principal rooms, and there were many expressions of admiration for the gracious house.

Afterwards, they adjourned to the cool shade of the rear terrace. The gardens presented a charming picture and won more praise, although Geraldine's bright eyes turned constantly to the open French doors through which a procession of cats came and went. Leopold was on his very best behaviour, charming the older lady and doing all in his power to please Helena. "I should very much like to see the ruins, Mrs. Cliveden," he remarked, looking out across the sun-drenched gardens to where the tall chimneys of the old house lifted above the trees. "Dare I hope you will show them to me?"

'I hope I am not so foolish,' she thought, and said lightly, "I expect Rostyn would be pleased to do so whenever you wish. He is often over there."

"How nice," he murmured dryly, his eyes saying 'spoil sport!'

"Do I hear my name?"

They all turned, and Geraldine uttered a pleased little cry to see the invalid upright, if leaning heavily on his crutches. Helena and Mrs. Hammond had to feign equal surprise though they had no need to feign delight, and Rostyn beamed with pride through the chorus of congratulations.

Any restraints occasioned by their separation soon vanished. The servants brought wines and cakes, and the conversation swept along, Geraldine recounting the latest on-dits from Town, much to Mrs. Hammond's delight, and Leopold apprising them of the gyrations of the world of fashion, and exciting Emmett and Rostyn with the news that Napoleon was said to be bound for Moscow to pursue his ambitions in that direction. It had been a long time since Helena had seen her brother so jolly and animated. He could scarcely keep his eyes from Geraldine, and noting that young lady's shy glances and the blushes that came and went in her sweet face, Helena thought them ideally suited. How nice it would be if they made a match of it.

Echoing her thoughts, Savage remarked, "I'd not have dreamed when last we met that I would find you so much improved today, Hammond. Gad, but this sylvan solitude and all the peace and quiet must be vastly beneficial."

"Much you know of it," grumbled Rostyn. "I am plagued to death in this 'sylvan solitude' as you call it. And as for peace and quiet—hah! My dear brother-in-law allows me none of that commodity!"

Mrs. Hammond laughed. "Cliveden sought to interest Rostyn in veterinary medicine, and he actually lured a few trusting souls to bring their creatures here."

"A few is it?" exclaimed her son, indignant. "I'll have you know, Mama, I've seen ten patients this week! In fact, I have a surgery, which," he turned to Geraldine, "I would like to show you, ma'am."

Geraldine looked at Savage pleadingly. "May I, Leo?"

"Only upon the condition that I am not asked to accompany you."

Geraldine jumped up and Helena crossed to the bell pull so as to summon Daniels and the invalid chair. Before she reached the pull however, Cliveden walked in. He was still wearing his travelling dress and looked tired and rather grim. "It would seem that I come just as everyone is leaving," he said, his gaze flickering from Geraldine to her brother. "I'd not known you expected to set out covers for company, m'dear."

Irked by the edge of displeasure in his voice, Helena restrained the impulse to remark that *she'd* not known he expected to go to London, and instead said coolly, "Miss Savage and her brother were at the Fete, and they were kind enough to agree to dine with us this evening."

Cliveden offered the appropriate comments, but his bows were stiff, his manner glacial. He made no attempt to go and change into evening clothes, but remained beside Helena, watching Savage—as Mrs. Hammond later observed—with the air of a bulldog guarding his new bone from the advance of the neighbour's hound.

Rostyn summoned Daniels and was wheeled off with Geraldine beside the chair, to inspect his "surgery" in the old house. Mrs. Hammond and Helena struggled to keep the conversation going, but Cliveden argued with every remark Savage made, and seemed bent on provoking a quarrel. Savage, who would normally have delighted in some verbal jousting, was all suave diplomacy, thwarting his aggressive host at every turn, and refusing to take up the challenges contained in Cliveden's scathing comments. By the time Rostyn and a starry-eyed Geraldine returned, Helena was much embarrassed, and so irked with her husband she could have boxed his ears. Savage, however, seemed more amused than annoyed. Cliveden waited until the last possible moment to rush upstairs and change. Soon afterwards Helena led her guests into the withdrawing room, and Mrs. Hammond slipped away to see to her cats. Rostyn lost no time in engaging Geraldine in low-voiced conversation, and Savage was as prompt in taking his place beside Helena on the blue velvet sofa that so nicely complemented her ice-blue gown.

"Well now, Milady Fair," he murmured. "And what has put your spouse's back up, I wonder?"

She turned to him repentantly. "Mr. Savage, I do apologize. Perhaps some matter of business has disturbed him. I am very sure he does not mean to be so abrupt, but—"

"But of course he does," he said with his cynical grin. "He is hoping very much that I become so offended as to make some plausible excuse and carry my sister away. Does he not approve of her infatuation with Hammond?"

Her heart gave a little leap. "Do you?"

"What have I to say to the matter? Geraldine is no longer a child, and with my father's approval will have whomsoever she chooses."

"You have a great deal to say and you know it. Gerry loves you deeply and would never marry to disoblige you. *Should* you be disobliged if she chose my brother?"

He gave an exaggerated sigh. "Alas, I strive to be polite and you will have nothing but the truth. Very well, ma'am. I think my sister is a *rara avis* and would be a fool to throw herself away upon a penniless cripple."

The colour drained from Helena's cheeks and she started up, infuriated. He caught her hand. "But conversely ma'am, Hammond is a gallant soldier, a most personable gentleman, certainly not a fortune-hunter, and his family is—" he leaned nearer, smiling his twisted smile "—is ... delicious."

Helena could not restrain a chuckle. "Villain," she said.

"But what a pretty scene," sneered Cliveden from the doorway.

Releasing the small hand he held, Savage drawled, "Well it was, dear boy. *Had* you to come back so very quickly?"

"I've a notion it is as well I did." Cliveden's eyes shot sparks as they rested on Helena. "Perhaps you should be tidying your hair, ma'am."

"But how unkind," murmured Savage. "Your wife's hair is perfectly glorious. Are you blind, Peter?"

Through his teeth Cliveden growled, "Very far from it. So have a care!"

"Cliveden!" exclaimed Helena, mortified.

"I think you overlook the fact that I am here also." Rostyn ignored the glare that was hurled at him, and went on, "And if you think me powerless to prevent this rascal from flirting with my sister, you must not have seen how well I go on with the crutches you—uh, so kindly brought me."

His guns effectively spiked by the unexpected warmth of his brother-in-law's smile, Cliveden bit his lip and watched as the crutches were demonstrated. Rostyn made his precarious way across the room, and started back, tired but elated. "There," he panted. "Now what have you to say to—"

The door burst open behind him and Emmett rushed in, Wagger bounding beside him. Geraldine screamed a warning, but the boy was unable to stop in time, and caromed into his wavering brother, sending the crutches flying.

Cliveden was very fast and steadied Rostyn, then turned on the boy angrily. "What the deuce are you thinking of, to rush into a room in such hobbledehoy

fashion? You came near to knocking your brother
down."

"He didn't mean it," muttered Rostyn, as Cliveden helped him to a chair.

"Even so, Cliveden is perfectly right," said Helena, her face pale with fright. "You must make your
apologies, Emmett."

"I—I do, indeed I do," stammered the boy. "I am
most terribly sorry, Ross. I would not have hurried so,
only—it is the news that has come." His eyes blazed
with excitement. He said ringingly, "The most awful
thing!"

Quick to be apprehensive, Geraldine asked, "Oh,
what is it? Not Wellesley?"

"No, no. His lordship's well, ma'am. It is the Prime
Minister!"

"And can be discussed when the ladies leave us,"
said Cliveden, frowning.

"What, and imagine disasters all through our dinner?" put in Rostyn. "Our young ladies are well out
of the schoolroom and I doubt politics will unnerve
either of 'em. Speak up, Emmett. What blunder has
Mr. Perceval managed now?"

The boy looked uneasily at Cliveden's scowl, but
then said with ghoulish relish, "A madman assassi-
nated him in the House of Commons this morning!"

"Good God!" exclaimed Rostyn, turning pale.

Helena and Geraldine arose with cries of horror.
Cliveden went at once to put his arm around his wife.
"No!" she gasped. "Oh, say it is not true!"

"It is, it is," declared Emmett, big with importance. "He was shot in front of the entire House, and—"

"No, no. It was in the Lobby," drawled Savage. Frightened as always by needless violence, Helena shrank against Cliveden. "Poor man! Oh, how dreadful. Is he—dead?"

"Yes. Almost immediately, so I heard." Cliveden tightened his arm about her. "I saw no point in upsetting you with such news."

Geraldine asked, "When did you learn of it, Leo?"

"This afternoon, when I was talking to the fellows in the curricle race. Which reminds me, one of 'em was an old acquaintance of yours, Hammond. Robert Eastleigh. To say truth, I was rather surpri—"

"Leo!" cried Geraldine, her dismayed glance flying to her friend.

For an instant, Helena felt as if time had stopped, leaving her in a frozen state, unable to move or speak. Vaguely, she knew that Cliveden's frame had jolted as though he'd been struck a violent blow. She heard him whisper her name, but still she could not speak.

Genuinely aghast, Savage muttered, "Oh, Gad! Don't she know?"

Mrs. Hammond hurried into the room. "Have you heard about—Oh, I see you have! Is it not ghastly? Helena, my love, you look positively ill!"

Cliveden said huskily, "My dear, come upstairs and rest. I'll—"

Gently but firmly, Helena detached herself from his arm. She did not know that her face was paper white,

her eyes great dark pools of shock. She said, "Ross—
is it truth? Is—is Robert Eastleigh still alive?"

"What?" screamed Mrs. Hammond.

Rostyn answered uneasily, "Uh—well—uh, that is
to say—"

"Helena," said Cliveden. "Please come, and let
me—"

She turned and looked steadily into his troubled
eyes. "Is—Eastleigh—still—alive?"

His hands clenched. He took a deep breath. "Yes.
But—"

"Oh! My *heavens*," whispered Mrs. Hammond,
wringing her hands.

"I am so glad." Helena smiled serenely at her
guests. "Shall we go in to dinner?"

ALONE AT LAST, Helena sat by her parlour fireplace,
staring blindly at the empty hearth. Most of the past
five hours were lost to her. She was told later that she
was calm and behaved with perfect propriety at the
dinner table, but she was conscious only of an inter-
val in which people spoke with grave, echoing voices,
faces seemed blurred and unreal, and there was a
quivering tension in the air. As in a dream she had led
the ladies from the table. When the gentlemen joined
them, the conversation was forced and often lan-
guished, and very soon after the tea tray was carried
in, Savage had taken his sister home.

Clearer than all else she remembered Cliveden
standing at the foot of the stairs, holding her candle,
and looking so drawn and haggard. He had tried very
hard to convince her to go straight to bed, but at last

had agreed to come in and talk for a minute or two before he retired.

As soon as she was in her nightrail and her hair taken down and brushed out, Helena had sent Emma off to bed, and had sat down, waiting.

After the initial shock, the enormous sense of gratitude and relief that Robert was not dead, so many questions had begun to creep into her mind. How was he? Not ill evidently, if he could participate in a curricle race from London to Brighton. But he must have been seriously wounded, else Cliveden would not have thought him dead. She knit her brows. Cliveden's wounds had been serious, and even now it was doubtful that he could compete in a curricle race. Of course, dear Robert had always been sporting mad, and he was so very well built and athletic. She closed her stinging eyes. Why had she not been told of his survival? It was typical of his high sense of gallantry that he would keep away now that she was married; knowing he could not in honour approach her. But surely he could at least have visited them? A morning call perhaps, if only to see how Rostyn went on, or to pay his respects to them all for the old friends they were.

Unless... Good heavens! He probably despised her! He had trusted her to remain true to him, and instead had come home wounded and ill, to find she had married another man! She gave an involuntary moan of anguish and bowed her head into her hands, weeping. *Why* had she rushed into this marriage like any panicked idiot? Why had she not had more *faith*? Why hadn't she waited just a little longer? Oh, if *only* she had waited!

After a while she dried her tears and strove for calm. She had acted in the way that had seemed best at the time. In so doing she'd ruined her life and hurt the man she loved, but it was done, and tears would not mend matters. It would be cruel to betray her grief to Cliveden, for she was more and more inclining to the belief that he had formed a tendre for his unwanted bride, and she would not hurt him for the world.

She heard soft footsteps in the hall, and quickly blew out all the candles but one. Dear Robert was alive; that was the only important thing. Pulling back her shoulders, she stood and turned to greet her husband.

The face that peeped around the opening door, however, was that of her youngest brother. "May I come in for a minute?" he asked apprehensively.

"Of course. Are you worrying about Ross?" She drew him into the cozy room. "He knew it was just an accident, and he is quite all right."

Emmett was wearing a scarlet dressing gown over his nightshirt, the sleeves showing signs of being outgrown. He sat beside her on the little sofa, peering into her face anxiously. "It's not that. You've been crying."

She managed a tremulous smile. "A little It's—just my silliness, do not regard it."

"No, it's not. It's because Mr. Savage said that about Eastleigh."

Helena held her breath, but before she could respond the boy rushed on. "You didn't know he'd come home, did you?"

"No," she whispered, trying to be sensible. "Did you?"

"Well, Bilge is his nephew y'know, and he told me about the fight."

Something very cold closed around Helena's heart. She stared at Emmett blankly. 'Bilge...' That would be the Honourable Felix Badgley, son of Robert's eldest sister, and currently also at Harrow. "Fight...?" she echoed numbly.

"Well, it wasn't much of a fight, I suppose. But Bilge said that Lord Robert was in a flame and that Cliveden rang a proper peal over him. Lord Robert said he'd not strike a man who was scarce able to stand up straight, and said some—other things about you getting married, so that Cliveden hit him anyway. Bilge said there would have been a proper turn-up, only his mama's servants (Bilge's mama, I mean) ran between them and called for Cliveden's people to come and take him away.

Her mind spinning, Helena said in a far-away voice, "And this all happened *before* we were married? You are very sure, Emmett?"

"Yes. Because—" His brow puckered. "Oh, I remember! Because Cliveden was still hobbling about with his cane then, and besides, Bilge said Eastleigh's great-uncle Burtonbrook sent Lord Robert to his shooting box in Lincolnshire and said he was not to come back 'til after your wedding."

So Cliveden had *known* Robert was alive! Helena gave a little gasp. How utterly *contemptible*! He had lied to her from the very first. Someone was patting her hand. Her eyes focused on her brother's anxious face. She asked, "Emmett dear, why did you not tell me all this long ago?"

"I was going to," he said reluctantly. "Only... I thought—Well, anyway, I did tell Ross when I came home for your wedding, and he said I was to say nothing because Lord Burtonbrook was right. It would only cause a lot of trouble and a fine scandal, and make everyone unhappy. So I didn't. And afterwards—" he gave a wry shrug "—I expect I forgot."

"I see." It all fell neatly into place. Cliveden's insistence upon an immediate and quiet marriage; the way he'd whisked them off to the country; the fact that they never entertained his Town friends. Small wonder Ross had been so contemptuous of him....

Emmett asked, "Have I done wrong, Nell? I'd not have told you, but you looked so funny when you heard Eastleigh was still alive. And I thought you might have—well, you know, had a—a passion for him or whatever they call that stuff. So I thought I'd better make a clean breast of it, and you can be cross with me, if you want to. Though," he added thoughtfully, "I'm not sure you really should be."

She hugged him, and assured him that she was not cross with him.

And after he'd gone she sat by the hearth again, her eyes very bright, and fury building inside her.

CHAPTER SEVEN

CLIVEDEN PAUSED OUTSIDE his wife's parlour and ran a nervous hand through his hair. From the beginning he'd known this moment would come, and he had dreaded it, guarded against it—until he was ready; until he was more sure of his ground. He should have known he would never be ready; never quite sure of his ground. Not in time. He scratched at the door and went inside.

Helena was standing at the window with her back to him. She wore a wrapper of pink stuff that billowed about her like a filmy cloud, and her glorious hair waved like gleaming brown silk about her shoulders. She turned, smiling, and although there was an odd blankness to the smile, he wondered if she knew how to look anything but exquisite, and for a moment he could not say a word but just stood there, staring.

"Thank you for coming, Cliveden," she said softly. "Pray sit down."

Instead, he walked straight to her. "You're tired. Cannot this wait 'til morning?"

She put out her hand, and he took it. How very small and white it was, and how deathly cold. His eyes sharpened. He said anxiously, "Are you well? I wish you will go to—"

"I am quite well, thank you." She walked around him to the little sofa. "It is just that I have had rather a shock."

She sat down. Uneasy, he watched the back of her head for a moment, then joined her, but no sooner was he seated than she stood and wandered about restlessly. "You did not tell me that you meant to go to London."

He did not at once answer. Then he said quietly, "I think you did not invite me here to discuss my reason for going to Town."

"And if I had, would you be honest with me?" She smiled, but there was no mirth in her smile. "How grim you look when you frown, Peter. And you do not answer me. Shall I guess why you went to Town? Did you steal away to see your—your light of love, my husband?"

He had never before seen her eyes glitter like this, and his fears deepened. "We reached an agreement when we married, and I have—"

"You have deceived me from the very start," she intervened, her usually gentle voice sharp with accusation.

He came to his feet. "I told you I admired another lady, and—"

"And you told me that the gentleman to whom I was betrothed was dead!"

It was said. The gauntlet was thrown. There followed a breathless pause, through which they faced each other unmoving.

Cliveden walked to stand with one hand on the mantelpiece. Gazing down at the gleaming andirons, he said, his voice strained, "Mistakes happen in warfare, Helena. Many people thought him killed."

"But you knew he was not."

He jerked around. "Why do you say that?" She drifted closer, her loveliness enhanced by the two spots of colour that glowed high on her cheekbones. "*When* did you know, Peter?"

Desperate, he seized her hand, and evaded, "Helena—my Helena, do you remember that first night I met you?"

"Not very well." She wrenched free and said contemptuously, "Robert was with me, you see, and I have a strange nature. When I am with the one I love, I scarcely notice any other man." He flinched to those bitter words, and she demanded again, "*When,* Cliveden? When did you learn that Robert was alive?"

His drew a hand across his eyes. "What difference does it make?"

"It might make a difference perhaps, if you had really believed him dead. *Did* you believe that, Mr. Cliveden? Or was it perhaps that—from the very beginning—you *knew* he was alive?" Her lip curled. "Now *that* would be really despicable! I think I could never forgive a man who would stoop so—low."

He sprang to seize her by the arms, crushing her against him with hands of steel. "You think you loved Eastleigh!" he snarled, his narrowed eyes blazing down into her wide startled ones. "But you don't know what it means to *really* love. To care for someone so much that you would gladly die for their dear sake, or would move heaven and earth to win them. In the first instant I saw you I loved you, my Helena. I could not get you out of—''

"Do not *dare* to call me that!" She beat her little fists against his chest, fighting to free herself. "I am not—nor will I ever be *your* Helena! You did not win me! You knew you could not, and so you determined to steal me away from the man *I* loved! The man who loved *me*! *Our* love meant nothing to you! You cared only for what *you* wanted. How could you *do* so vile a thing? How *could* you lie and cheat without a—''

His voice harsh with anguish he broke in, "For the love of God—try to understand! When you were in such need, I thought—''

"You saw your chance, you mean! Your chance to take advantage of my grief and helplessness! You deceived me. And—and *bought* me!''

"No!" White as death, he reached for her again, but she ran back a few steps, pulling her garments closer about her.

His hand fell. He sighed, "Very well. I won't touch you. Only, please—if you will just listen—''

"Listen to more of your lies? Oh, you were wounded, but not so gravely that Robert was obliged to save your life. You invented the whole sickening tale only to trick me into believing that he was killed so that you might then appear to be nobly fulfilling an obligation of honour by offering for me. *That's* the truth—yes?''

One hand clenched. He said hoarsely, "To an extent—yes.''

Somehow, deep in her heart had lingered a glimmer of hope that there would be some reasonable explanation. His words closed the door on hope, and she shrank, regarding him with shuddering revulsion.

"Don't look at me like that! Helena—I *love* you! I only wanted to care for and protect you!"

"If you truly loved me you would not have made me suffer the pain I lived through when I believed Robert killed. How could you be so selfish? Did it never occur to you that sooner or later I would meet him? And that when I did—" She broke off, her eyes widening. "Oh!" she gasped. "*That* was why you would never let me go to Town! You were afraid I might see him!"

He offered no defence, but stood with head bowed before her scorn.

Helena ran to open the hall door. "Be so good as to leave my room."

He walked slowly to the door, but then wrenched it from her hand and closed it again. "What do you mean to do?"

"Leave." At that, he looked so grim that she was afraid, but she went on disdainfully, "You have schemed and plotted to no avail, sir. I will no longer be your wife."

He said dryly, "You never have been, save in the eyes of the law."

"Then the eyes of the law shall be opened. We must have a Bill of Divorcement, Mr. Cliveden."

"Never!" His chin jerked up. "I'll have no scandal for the gabblemongers to gloat over!"

"Nothing must taint your honourable name, is that it, sir? And what of your own obligations to that name? Can you be proud of what you have done?"

A little nerve was throbbing at his temple. "No," he half-whispered. "But, we have made an agreement, and I do not intend to—"

"To give up your investment in me? Yes, I suppose we must in fairness consider what I cost you. Mama's bills, Emmett's fees, our—"

It seemed to her that he shrank, and one hand lifted slightly, as if to ward off a blow. "No... Do not... I beg."

Suddenly, Helena could not seem to see clearly. She wiped angrily at her eyes, but went on in a less scathing tone, "No. I—I am being vulgar. I apologize. I thought, you see, that—whatever else—I had married a man of honour. But I cannot continue to be your wife, Mr. Cliveden, even in name only. You must give me a divorce. Surely you see it is the only way."

He raised his head and looked at her, and she thought she had never seen so haggard and despairing a face, but when he spoke his voice was firm. "It is the way I will not take, ma'am. My parents return from India this winter. My mama is a true gentlewoman, and my father is the kindest and best of men. They both are proud of our name and—and of me. I'll not have them come home to disgrace. No, there is no use to argue. I'll not consider it."

"Whether or not you 'consider it' they *will* be returning to disgrace!"

"Perhaps. But it will not be aired in public."

"I see." Proudly scornful, she said, "You cannot keep me here by force. I have my brothers to defend me, thank God! I shall go back to London."

He gazed at the little slipper that peeped from beneath her wrapper. "Very well. I will have the London house made ready, if that is what you wish. For a while, however, we must keep together. You need have no fears. I will not—" his mouth twisted "—demand the rights I have never known."

"Thank you." She opened the door once more, and stared through him icily.

He stepped into the hall, then turned back. "Helena," his voice broke. "I know that—that what I did was very bad, but—please—can you not try to understand? To—forgive?"

"I was so very grateful to you," she said in a flat, remote voice. "I think I could have forgiven you almost anything. My Papa held that any gentleman who stoops to tell a lie is beneath contempt. But you sank even lower! You lied so as to come between me and the man I loved. You broke his heart—as well as mine. *En effet* you have ruined three lives, Mr. Cliveden. And that—I cannot forgive."

THE WIND WHICH HAD COME UP earlier in the evening died away soon after one o'clock, and the night was very quiet. But despite the hush, so conducive to slumber, one occupant of Whisperwood slept not at all that night. His mind was haunted by the image of two great dark eyes that flashed with disgust; in his ears rang the words that still seemed to sear his very soul; and in his heart was a crushing despair.

Along the corridor, her door securely locked, another wakeful occupant lay huddled and forlorn, weeping softly for hopes shattered and love lost; and who suffered another pain every bit as sharp—the pain of disillusionment.

LONDON WAS BUSY AND COLOURFUL, vibrant with the sounds and smells and excitements of late spring. The social calendar was crowded with balls and musicales, routs, teas, breakfast and boat parties, and every possible entertainment to chase away boredom. Everyone who was anyone was caught up in the merry whirl, and the Season was rated more sparkling than ever by reason of the emergence of several new Toasts. Among these beauties was the dashing young Mrs. Cliveden, who, although well born, had been lost to the public eye before her marriage, but was now to be seen everywhere and much admired for her beauty and elegance. Only recently wed, she was so fortunate as to possess that most desirable of husbands, a gentleman of retiring habits who went his own ways and showed little interest in the activities of his bride. The Town beaux worshipped at her shrine—all the more willing to flirt with a lovely lady who was also safely wed. The single girls watched her enviously, their jealousy the less vitriolic since she posed no threat to their own matrimonial prospects. The matrons acknowledged her beauty, but viewed with scepticism her meteoric rise to social prominence.

Typical of the latter were two stately dowagers who left the crowded ballroom at Francklyn House one warm June evening, and retreated to a sofa in the cooler hall. Here, they indulged in some delicious character assassination while sipping iced punch.

"The Cliveden," allowed Mrs. Blanck, in response to her companion's remark, "has a passable figure I grant you, my dear Amy."

"And a magnificent wardrobe," sighed Mrs. Hopewell, wishing her daughter was less partial to the sweets which had such a deplorable effect upon her waistline. "Cliveden must dote on her to permit that she spends so lavishly. Did you see the gown she wore to Drury Lane last night? And those diamonds?"

"I saw them, and you saw them. The question is, did her husband see them? If Cliveden dotes on her, he'd best do it a touch more visibly."

"Already? But they're only just wed!"

Mrs. Blanck shrugged. "It would be hard to say who's the bigger fool. Her, for jauntering about with every man save her charming young husband. Him, for allowing it. There may be nothing to it, of course, but—". She leaned nearer and said with ponderous drama, "There are—*whispers*, Amy!"

Her friend wriggled with delight. "How dreadful! Who, Mildred?"

"Bainbridge writes odes to her eyes, so I hear; young Redditch is at her feet; St. Jacques is so besotted it is positively revolting to see him mooning; and Savage hovers like a hawk preparing to swoop."

"Good heavens! Then Cliveden had best call her to heel before he's obliged to call Savage out! I'd not want that one hovering over *my* girl!"

Mrs. Blanck, with three unmarried daughters to fire off, knit her brows and said thoughtfully, "He's a rake, I'll own. But he has a certain charm, Amy."

"Perhaps, but—" Mrs. Hopewell edged a little nearer and dropped her carefully hoarded and tasty bombshell. "Did you know that Eastleigh is back in Town? I fancy *he'll* soon be fluttering about the chit! They were betrothed before Cliveden whisked her to the altar, you know. And I am sure you have heard..." She bent to the eager ear of her confidante.

Mrs. Blanck listened, and nodded grimly. "Small wonder he is no longer seen anywhere. He likely knows the entire town is aware of his dishonourable behaviour."

At this precise moment a vision in a silvery-pink gown rapped her fan lightly upon the knuckles of her escort. "You are wicked, Leo," she said, but with a smile. "I shall do no such thing. Mrs. Gallen's card parties have notoriously high stakes, and I am quite out of pin money."

Savage leaned across the table in the crowded supper room, his blue eyes alight as he squeezed Helena's hand. "Yes, because you spent it all on that gown, you naughty puss. And, Gad, if ever I saw anything so delicious. That frosted blush becomes you beyond bearing. Come—give me the pleasure of your company. And never worry for your losses. I'll stake you, m'dear."

She gave a little ripple of laughter, and withdrew her gloved hand from his clasp. "Cliveden would beat me if I committed such an indiscretion. And how did you know this colour is called Frosted Blush?"

He caught up the trailing end of her zephyr shawl and bound it about his forehead. "I look into my crystal ball," he intoned sonorously. "It sees all, knows all!" Several amused glances came their way, and he added with a twinkle, "Enough to know you care not a fig for what Cliveden thinks. Besides which, if he hasn't beaten you by now, wicked one, he should have!"

She snatched her shawl away and said tartly, "Your wife will have my deepest sympathy, Leopold."

"If I cannot have *you*, Fairest, I shall have no wife! But I have vexed you, as usual. How can I—"

He broke off. Helena was staring past him, her face perfectly white.

Savage turned quickly. Robert Eastleigh, very handsome in evening dress, stood watching Helena, his face grave.

Scowling, Savage said, "Nell—come back upstairs and—"

"No," she interrupted shakily. "Please go away, Leo."

He gripped her wrist hard. "You know that I adore you, and bitterly regret that I let Cliveden win you. But I'll not be a party to—"

Eastleigh said in his beautifully modulated voice, "I believe the lady asked you to leave, Savage."

Ignoring him, Savage murmured urgently, "Don't be a fool, Nell. Come. Before the gossips start their tattling!"

"Leo," Helena's eyes pleaded, "I *must* talk with him! Be kind to me."

Well aware that many watched them, Savage hesitated, then pushed back his chair. Obligingly, Eastleigh tugged at it. Savage glanced through him as if he were not there, and strolled away, cursing under his breath as he heard the little buzz of excited comment.

Eastleigh heard it also and offered his arm. Without a word, Helena stood and rested her hand on it and they left the supper room as the conversation level rose abruptly.

Her heart pounding, Helena was scarcely conscious of walking, but somehow they were on the rear terrace, and Eastleigh was closing the French doors behind them. He turned to her. She had time only to say a tremulous, "Robert..." before he swept her into his arms and murmured throatily, "My darling! My lovely one!" Then, she was being kissed until her breath was gone and her knees were blancmange. Dizzied, she clung to him while he kissed his way down her throat.

"No!" She managed somehow to pull away. "Robert—I am ... married!"

"By trickery and deception! But you belong to me, and always will!" He drew her to a secluded stone bench behind some potted shrubs. "You know what happened?" he asked, pressing kisses onto her gloved fingers.

"No. My—I was told you were killed. I was frantic."

"And victimized, poor darling! I was hit and knocked down merely. Couldn't quite recall who I was for a little, so they shipped me off to hospital. When I came home I was told you were about to be married. To Cliveden! God! I refused to believe it! I almost ran mad!"

Tears slipping down her cheeks, she stroked his bowed head tenderly. "Dearest, why did you not come for me? Had I dreamed you were alive—"

He groaned. "Of all the prize fools, I told Uncle Ajax I'd kill Cliveden before I'd let him have you, and the old curmudgeon at once sent me packing to the Shires. He said he was afraid for my health. I know damned well it was scandal he was afraid of! I came to you just as soon as I returned."

"But—but you were in Sussex a month ago. Leo Savage said—"

"Oh, he told you about the curricle race, did he? Well, that happened to suit my purpose. I'd intended to drive down and seek you out anyway, but I was obliged to complete the race." He gave a rueful grin. "Be dashed if I didn't turn the blasted curricle over, and knock myself up again!"

"Oh—poor Robert! Such a time you have had!"

She was seized and passionately kissed. She had yearned for this, but now the embraces she should have gloried in were tainted by a niggling guilt, and she pushed him away. "Robert, you must not! If we should be seen!"

"They'll see me with you often enough, I promise you! That unprincipled trickster may think he has stolen away my lady, but he's a lot to learn!" He saw dismay in her lovely face, and went on grimly, "I cannot bear to think of the hell he has put you through!"

"I grieved for you, Robert. Oh, so much I grieved! But, in his own way, he cares for me. And—and he was very kind to Ross and my family."

"Filthy scheming bas—"

"Robert!"

He groaned again, and smothered her hands with kisses. "Forgive, my Fair. I am quite distracted! To find you again . . . to see your sweet face, after all this misery. If you but knew how I've suffered!"

"I do know," she cried, melting into his embrace once more. "Oh, beloved, I *do* know! How grateful I am that you are alive!"

"Much good that does me, without you as my wife! Nell—have you asked him for a divorce?"

She could see Cliveden's stricken face again, and she flinched a little, and nodded. "He flatly refuses."

"Conniving worm! I knew he'd never let you go!"

Laughing voices were approaching. Helena gave a gasp of fear, and jumped up. "I must go!"

He stood and caught her arm. "Not until you tell me when I can see you again. Do you ride in the Park?"

The voices were closer. She pushed him away desperately. "Yes, Robert—you're hurting me!"

He kissed her wrist tenderly. "Tomorrow. At seven. I'll find you!"

She fled.

Eastleigh stood gazing after her. He started as a lady and two gentlemen came up the terrace steps then paused, looking from him to the swirl of a pink gown disappearing through the door. "Oh! Er—Good evening," said Eastleigh, obviously flustered. They all stared. Rather ostentatiously straightening his neckcloth he strode around the side of the house.

"Well I never," murmured the lady.

One of the gentleman tittered. "You're surely not surprised? We've all been waiting for it. There are some sizeable bets on the books, in fact."

The other gentleman said with a frown, "Deuced bad form. I wonder how Peter Cliveden will explain matters to his father. Don't envy him."

"No, indeed," said the lady as they walked on. "And I heard..."

NOT RELISHING THIS INTERVIEW, Cliveden went quietly into his bride's bedchamber. It would be morning for only another half hour, yet there was no movement from the graceful canopied bed. He walked over to it and gently drew back the curtains. Delilah and Soot, two of the three cats they had not left in Sussex, blinked up at him. Delilah gave a soft trill, and Cliveden stroked her absently. Helena lay on her back, her head turned to one side, her long eyelashes like small curved fans against her flushed cheeks. Her nightcap was halfway down one ear, her hair a tumbled mass, her rosy lips slightly parted. Watching her, Cliveden's eyes became wistful. How bewitching she was; how very exquisite and dear and desirable...

Delilah decided to be playful and began to pedal furiously at his hand.

Half asleep still, Helena stirred, pushing the covers away. She wore a nightdress that was an enticing drift of filmy lavender silk, with a dainty lace yoke that plunged almost to the waist. As she moved, one of the narrow shoulder straps slipped, revealing so lovely a sight that Cliveden gave a gasp, and his grip on the bedcurtain caused the upper rail to jerk. Helena's head turned on the pillow, and she sighed. He retreated to stand staring blindly out of the window to where First Cat was ignoring the temptation posed by a recklessly strutting London pigeon. She was his wife, thought Cliveden, so there was no cause for him to feel like a Peeping Tom, but—He tensed. Helena was talking drowsily.

"...Funny old world, Delilah. I thought, you know, when we came to London that if I could not be happy, at least I knew just where I stood and everything would run along in an orderly way. Well—" a faint sigh "—it ran along. But now I am more disordered than ever. To be a Toast, dear Soot, is a bore. Who would ever think it?" A yawn. "Do you miss the clean quiet country, my dears? Do you miss your friends, and...that dear old house?" (Cliveden's guilty heart began to pound wildly.) "If we go back, Rostyn will be so glad to see us. But...would *he* come also, do you think?" A heavier sigh this time. Frowning, Cliveden knew he must end this.

"I think you should know," he drawled, hearing her shocked gasp, "that I cannot help but hear your rather one-sided conversation."

Helena's head shot out from between the curtains that she pulled tightly shut under her chin. "Infamous!" she cried indignantly. "Do you add eavesdropping to your questionable accomplishments, sir?"

He offered an ironic bow. "We must discuss a few matters, and your—er, erratic hours make it difficult to arrange an interview."

"I suppose that means you are angry because I stay out late."

He thought her scowl almost too adorable to be resisted, but managed to say mildly, "It is not the hour, but the—er, company, to which I object."

She'd been expecting this, and inwardly she trembled a little. "You have your friends, Mr. Cliveden. I have mine."

"I think I do not flaunt with my 'friends' under the eyes of the ton."

"Perhaps you are ashamed of the company you keep. I am not!"

She looked absurdly young and little with just her head sticking out and her nightcap askew. A twinkle came into his eyes. "Helena, I really would prefer to see all of you while we talk."

"You probably did, while I was sleeping," she accused, not really believing it to be true.

His glance fell away and his cheeks reddened.

"You *did!*" Forgetting herself, she sprang from the bed and advanced on him in a flame. "You dared to peep at me while I slept! Is there *nothing* you will not stoop—" And she checked, the look in his eyes suddenly reminding her of her very revealing attire. "Oh.. !" she said feebly, and threw up one hand to try and compensate for the plunging neckline.

It was probably because her hand was thus trapped when he seized her, she reasoned later, that she was able to put up so little resistance. Her squeaked, *"Cliveden!"* resulted in nothing but a hungry growl. Then his lips clamped down on hers. His kisses were quite different to Robert's, but even more brutal. Every time he came up for air, she got no farther than a gasped, "Beast!" or "Brute!" before her words were ruthlessly cut off. He kissed her lips until she was too breathless to object, then turned his attention to her cheeks, and her eyelids (which made her shiver), and her throat, and—elsewhere (which made her shiver even more). And when she tried to apprise him of his utter lack of decency, he caught her up and threw her on the bed. That brought her denunciation to an abrupt halt, and she lay there, watching him with wide frightened eyes.

"I have been very patient with you, Helena," he panted, hands clenched at his sides.

"You—pr—promised it was a—a *mariage de convenance*," she quavered. "Haven't you brought me enough misery? Do promises mean n-nothing to you?"

"My good name means something to me. I'll not have you drag it in the dust, my girl!"

She sat up, pulling the coverlet around her near nakedness. "Only because I have set up my court—"

"Court—hell!" Hands on hips, eyes dark and stormy, he towered over her. "I care not two farthings for the likes of St. Jacques and Bainbridge and the rest of 'em. And for all his reputation, Savage is a gentleman. But Eastleigh I'll not stand for, Helena! These past ten days you've set the town on its ears. End it. Now. If I find you have been with him again—"

"*Been* with him?" she echoed, stiffening. "How exactly am I to interpret that uncouth remark?"

His hand shot out to grab the edges of the coverlet and wrench her up to him. With his lips a breath away from her own, he said very softly, "It had better be the same interpretation as my own, madam! Or—so help me God, he'll answer to me—and we shall really give old London Town a scandal!"

An odd whiteness was around his mouth; a never before glimpsed steely glare lit the grey eyes. Afraid, she tried to hide it and laughed shrilly. "A duel? Robert is an excellent shot, Mr. Cliveden. Have a care!"

His lip curled. "Is that a threat, ma'am?"

"Oh! How *dare* you!"

"Stay away from Robert Eastleigh—or you'll see what I would dare!" He turned and marched to the door.

She called after him, "Only to protect your precious family honour? Do you really think you have any left?"

He said over his shoulder, "There is one way for you to make sure, but I doubt you would find the consequences worth the escapade."

As soon as his footsteps died away, Helena ran to her mirror. Her face was reddened here and there where his horrid cheek had scraped her tender skin. Her lips felt bruised. She touched them very softly, and her fingers wandered to the other places he had kissed. She met her eyes in the mirror, and blushed, then covered her face. He was typically inconsistent. One minute his eyes were like Toledo steel—the next, they were all adoring tenderness. How cruelly strong his arms had been. Her poor ribs were likely forged together. And the dishonourable wretch had ogled her while she lay sleeping! She peeped through her fingers. It really was a very pretty nightdress. . . .

CHAPTER EIGHT

"THE AUCTION IS AT half past two, exactly." Cliveden pulled off his gauntlets as he walked across the sunny hall beside Helena. She had seemed to enjoy their morning ride, and, encouraged, he said, "I would not impose upon your time twice in one day, ma'am, but my Uncle Ivan will be there to identify the piece for me, and he would be so pleased to see us together, in view of—"

"In view of all the gossip about your notorious bride," supplied Helena softly, accompanying him up the stairs. "What is it, may I ask?"

He said, poker faced, "Mostly about Eastleigh and Savage, but—"

"You know perfectly well," she put in with a toss of her curls, "that I referred to the piece your Papa has commissioned you to purchase for him."

"Oh." He grinned covertly. "It is a clock."

The wind had tousled his hair and brought a glow into his cheeks. He still limped, but his lean figure enabled him to wear his clothes well, and there was about him that aura she had not at first recognized, but now knew well; the hint of steel that lurked just below the quiet manner he showed to the world. He glanced at her and she looked away quickly. "A clock?"

"Yes. My mama collects them. She has yearned for this particular piece for years, and when my father heard that the collection was to be sold, he wrote asking me to buy the clock. He means to present it as his gift on their wedding anniversary." He smiled faintly. "Thirty-two years together... A truly happy marriage."

The sudden wistfulness in his eyes was reflected in her own. She sighed, "Such as I had hoped to enjoy."

He flushed, and his eyes hardened. "You will oblige me by being prompt, ma'am. I pledge to have you home in plenty of time to dress for the ball."

She promised to oblige, and went into her parlour, her heart leaping nervously. Tonight they would attend one of London's most eagerly anticipated events, the summer masquerade ball given by Sir Walter Wansford and his lady. Cliveden did not enjoy costume parties, but since the Wansfords were his neighbours in Sussex, he felt duty-bound to attend. He had not told Helena what he planned to wear, nor had she offered any information about her own costume.

In the bedchamber Emma was unwrapping a large box. She looked up and said an excited, "It's come, ma'am!"

"Oh," said Helena, half-wishing it had been lost somewhere. "No one saw it, did they?"

"No, Mrs. Cliveden." Emma unfolded the paper carefully, and held up the Egyptian Princess costume. "Oooh... It's so pretty! And only look at the wig! Oh, ma'am—so many plaits—it's enormous! The master will be so proud! Are you going to model it for him?"

"I certainly am not!" The girl shot a startled glance at her, and Helena added quickly, "It's to be a surprise, Emma. I teased Mr. Cliveden that he would never recognize me, and he was so sure of himself and said he'd know me anywhere, whatever I wore!"

The abigail chuckled. "Just like a man. But p'raps he would at that. It's clear to see he fair worships the ground you walk on."

Helena turned away hurriedly, holding the gown against her. It was a flowing creation of rich blue silk, with one shoulder bared. Braided gold ribbons formed the solitary shoulder strap, then continued to encircle the breasts and tie in at the waist. "Well," she said, thinking that it was a little more daring than she'd realized, "he shall have his chance tonight. I've told Cook to send my dinner up here and I shall slip out of the side door early. Miss Savage and her brother will take me up with them. When we get to the ball, we shall see if my husband recognizes me."

Emma grinned. "Who is the master to be, ma'am?"

"That is a surprise, too. But, it doesn't matter, for we will find each other at the unmasking, if not before. Now, you must promise to breathe not a word of all this, Emma."

"Not a word, ma'am! Even if he should chop me into gobbets!"

Helena laughed and said it was unlikely Mr. Cliveden would resort to *quite* such desperate measures. She thought, 'The wig is truly superb. He'll never know me! I will be perfectly safe!' And wondered why she felt more troubled than ecstatic.

THE AUCTION ROOMS WERE LOCATED in a large warehouse in Holborn. It was a rather grimy district but by the time the Clivedens arrived a large crowd had gathered. Lord Ivan Swann put Helena in mind of a big amiable sheep, who had apparently imbibed freely at his luncheon. He persisted in calling Helena 'Dorothy,' much to her husband's embarrassment, and frequently engaged his nephew in rambling and largely inarticulate conversation.

Helena had never been to a public auction before, and was much intrigued. She acquired a huge and very ugly cut-glass bowl when she waved to a friend, and was taken aback when Cliveden explained the various means by which one signalled the auctioneer. "I shall not so much as breathe until we leave!" she said, and would afterwards only speak to him in furtive whispers.

After a while, the Byeberry collection was offered and there was some spirited bidding. Cliveden bid on none of the exquisite clocks, but raised his hand when a small reproduction of a Spanish galleon was offered.

"That's not a clock!" hissed Helena. "Your mama likely wants that adorable little porcelain timepiece with the beautiful paintings."

"Oh, no she doesn't," he whispered, and eventually bought the ship for a sum which left his wife speechless.

When the auction ended, he took her over to view the galleon. "It was made in about 1585," he said, elated by his success. "Is it not superb workmanship?

Mark the carving of the aftercastle and the jewelled figures."

Inspecting the beautiful piece critically, Helena asked, "But how does one tell the *time*?"

He chuckled. "Ever the practical female! Here, m'dear. The dial is just below the middle mast. Now—watch the figures on the half-hour."

He drew her closer and so intrigued was she that she did not notice when his arm remained about her waist. The single hand on the dial moved to the line mid-way between four and five. There was a delicate chime, and the little group of sailors on the deck jerked to life and tottered about until they had exchanged places, whereupon they jerked into immobility once more.

Helena clapped her hands. "Oh! It is marvellous! And so old! Are those real jewels, Peter?"

He nodded, his eyes alight. "Mama will be in alt!"

"As would I!" Belatedly, she realized that she was leaning on his arm, and moved quickly away. "Goodness! If your galleon tells time accurately, it is half past four already! We must go. Shall they pack it up for you?"

"No. The sales must be registered and a certificate made out for us. I'll collect our purchases tomorrow." He asked whimsically, "Dare I beg that you wake my uncle while I make the arrangements?"

It was no easy task to awaken his lordship, and when she succeeded, Helena was inundated by his friendly but incomprehensible chatter. Politely smiling, her thoughts were far away. It had been some time since she'd seen such a light of happiness in Cliveden's sensitive face. She could almost hear Emma's voice: "It's clear to see he fair worships the ground you walk on." The prospect of a secret rendezvous with Robert this evening became even more troubling. She gave herself a mental shake. Perhaps Cliveden did love her, but it was a selfish and dishonourable love, and there was Robert to be considered. Dear faithful, loyal Robert.

"OH, BUT YOU LOOK RAVISHING, Nell," exclaimed the lady of the harem. "Only look at that wig! Cliveden will never recognize you, will he, Leo?"

Savage, who managed to be elegant even as a coalheaver, said ardently, "I'd know her, did she wear a sack over her head. What is Cliveden to be?"

"I don't know." Helena settled back against the squabs of the luxurious barouche. "It is so good of you to take me up."

"I am only glad we could be in Town again so that I might aid so glorious a lady," said Savage. "I'd to practically pry my sister from her rural haven. As though we weren't going to be there long enough this summer!"

Geraldine blushed, and Helena smiled and asked innocently, "How is my brother? He writes he is coming to Town, but does not say when."

"Tomorrow." Savage nudged her mischievously. "He has something of importance to discuss with your mama, I believe."

Helena gave a squeak. "Gerry! Oh—is it . . . ?"

Geraldine's shy smile was answer enough, and Helena hugged her. "I *could* not be more pleased! Now I shall have you for my sister! How splendid!"

Wiping away a grateful tear, Geraldine begged that Helena not divulge her awareness of the happy secret. "Rostyn wants to tell you himself, but refused to come tonight for fear he would be persuaded to attend this party."

Helena laughed. "Ross loathes fancy dress balls. Here we are, and only look at the crush. You do promise you won't betray me to Cliveden?"

"Only," said Savage, "if I am given three dances, fair one."

"Rascal. You'll have Cliveden up in arms."

He shuddered theatrically. "Two, then. Or I tell all!"

Amused, Helena's eyes were searching among the guests climbing the steps towards the open doors of the mansion. Robert was to be a Roman centurion and had promised to meet her in the hall.

An hour later she had still not found him. She had danced twice, and was now surrounded by a most determined group of oddities, including a King's Justice who said she was divine; a caveman who shouted poetry at her over the din; a matador and a Russian cossack, both pleading for her dance card; and a baker who insisted she was his goddess. The Justice was stout and no longer young; she couldn't believe Cliveden would wear the caveman costume, which was in questionable taste, but he could be any one of the others, for the crush was so great it was hard to tell if a man limped, and he could very easily have removed his ring. A beefeater was bearing down on her; the familiar figure of a coalheaver was pushing his way through the throng; a medieval Venetian nobleman was smiling at her as he approached and he had well-cut lips and even white teeth. She thought a panicked, 'Cliveden!'

A hand seized hers. She turned, startled, and encountered a masked Roman centurion, tall and splendid in high helm and tunic, his shapely legs protected from the knees down by bronze greaves.

"Thought I'd never find you." Eastleigh's voice was clipped. "Come."

Not waiting for her response, he shouldered the others aside, and when the caveman protested, snapped, "Stand away from my wife, fellow," so that the man drew back muttering embarrassed apologies. Dragged helplessly behind him, Helena was obliged to all but run, and drew several irked stares as she collided with those he pushed past. By the time they reached the side hall she was dishevelled and angry. Wrenching her hand away she said breathlessly, "I do not care to be made a spectacle, Robert!" She sent a lackey to fetch her cloak, and went on, "Had you come when you were supposed—"

"I was delayed. Cliveden didn't wait to catch us together, he simply caught *me* before I left! I handled him, never fear." He took the cloak the lackey brought and wrapped it around Helena. "My coach is in the alley."

"Are we going to your uncle's house?"

"No. He's coming to mine. Have you seen your charming spouse?"

"He *is* here then?"

"Probably." He flung open the side door. "Beastly fellow was in costume when he came to my flat. Took

me an age to get into this regalia after I was rid of
him." He said in a softer tone, "Not that it ain't worth
it to see you in that gown, Nell. Gad but you had all
the men at your pretty feet tonight!"

In the alley a closed coach waited, and Eastleigh
handed Helena inside, shouted to the coachman and
slammed the door. Before she could say a word, he
was kissing her passionately. She was too nervous to
be in the mood for his embraces, and pushed him
away, demanding, "What did Cliveden say?"

He scowled darkly. "I have been warned off, my
love. The gall of it! That lying conniver stole my lady
and now dares threaten me!"

"Threaten you! Oh, heavens! He didn't strike
you?"

He lifted her hand and kissed it tenderly. "How
touching that you worry for me. Do not, sweetheart.
I can handle the clod easily enough if he should come
the ugly. Which he won't. Not the type."

"I wonder. Sometimes I—I think he's a very dangerous man."

Eastleigh howled with mirth. "He has you properly hornswoggled, I see!"

"Perhaps. But you know what Society would make
of it, Robert. I am, after all, his wife, and sometimes
I cannot but see—"

"See what?" Quick to hear the uncertainty in her
voice, he peered at her bewitching profile touched by
the glow from the carriage lamps. "Dearest, you do
still love me? He hasn't won you away? I know what
a tricky swine he is. Playing on your sympathies when
he's not running to his precious Dorothy."

Helena felt as though she had been touched by an icy hand. "Dorothy? Lord Swann kept calling me that."

"Did he, by Jove! I'll wager Cliveden nigh strangled him! She's his mistress, my little innocent. I thought you knew."

With an effort, Helena kept her voice calm. "He had said he loved another. I told you that." She wished his laugh was not quite so loud.

"If he does, it cannot be that one, Nell," he said, still chuckling. "She's been his for years, but she's neither young nor pretty. Of course, Cliveden's such a block there's no expecting him to have good taste." Helena frowned but made no comment and there was a brief silence while the carriage wound through London's busy streets and the coachman exchanged insults with a carter whose slow-moving vehicle impeded their progress.

Love, thought Helena, was most odd. She had been shattered when she'd believed this dashing and gallant young man had been slain. Yet now that they were together at last, she could only feel depressed and vulgar. It must be because Cliveden was such a threat. Cliveden—who had so intensely declared his love for her, but had crept away to his adored, Dorothy...

Eastleigh enquired idly, "How came you to be with Ivan Swann? I think he seldom shifts his lazy carcass beyond his own door."

Helena pushed her husband from her thoughts, and told Eastleigh about the auction and the clock. "It was the very loveliest thing, Robert. The figures were jewelled and moved about. I never saw its like!"

"No more have I," he said, his thoughts elsewhere. "It sounds as if it should be under lock and key."

"I fancy it will be once he collects it. He has to go back and get it tomorrow, for there are papers to be made out, or some such thing."

Eastleigh sat up straighter. "Then that means you will be free for a while at least. Will he have far to go?"

"To Holborn only. The warehouse is an ugly old place, in a rather grim neighbourhood."

"Even so, you'll be able to get away." He pulled her into his arms. "We can meet in the park again. What time does he go?"

"I believe he said in the morning."

The chaise lurched to a stop before a tall house in Ryder Street.

Helena tidied her wig nervously. "Whatever will Lord Burtonbrook think of us for appealing to him when we both are in fancy dress?"

"He's a mere man, sweetheart; he'll be properly bowled out. Truly, you are so beautiful tonight I scarce can bear to let you out of my arms."

The footman opened the door and Eastleigh sprang down, then handed Helena onto the flagway. Ryder Street was deserted save for two very hilarious gentlemen who shouted questions as to when the lions were to be let loose.

Grateful for her mask, Helena took it off once they were inside. Eastleigh ushered her into a spacious flat to the right of the entrance and closed the door. She whispered, "Do you think he really can help us?"

"If he cannot, my lovely, then no one can. Carstairs?" he raised his voice, and a pale, sleek-looking servant appeared. "Has my uncle come?"

The servant bowed and imparted the information that his lordship had sent word he would be a trifle delayed.

Eastleigh grunted, and took Helena's arm. "In here, beloved."

The parlour was cosy and immaculate, its furnishings masculine but elegant. A small table near the fire was set with snowy napery and the gleam of silver and crystal. For two. Helena's eyes flew to Eastleigh.

Laughing at her, he took her hands and said soothingly, "Never fear, my doubting little love. I had no more in mind than a cozy supper and the chance to talk with you before my uncle arrives."

She allowed him to remove the cloak from her shoulders and give it to Carstairs. The servant's eyes flickered over her dispassionately, but she could scarcely endure to meet them. If he spoke of this, the disgrace to Cliveden was not to be thought of. Even if Lord Burtonbrook did come, she was here alone, without her husband, conduct far beyond the bounds of acceptable behaviour. She thought defiantly, 'And why not? What of Cliveden's conduct with his Dorothy? What's good for the goose...'

Eastleigh brought over two glasses of wine. "A toast! To our future!"

She smiled into his adoring eyes, but then was asking, "Robert—your man. Is he reliable?"

"With the reliability of self-preservation, sweetheart. I know enough about Mr. Edgar Carstairs to

have him transported at the very least. Come—drink
with me, heart of my life."

Stifling a small voice that asked why an honourable
gentleman would have a dishonourable servant, Helena sipped, then made a face. "What is this?"

"Madeira. You need it, dearest. I think your lovely
knees are knocking."

He led her to a small velvet sofa, sat close beside
her, and slipped one arm around her. For a few minutes they sat there in silence, gazing into the fire, his
fingertips stroking very gently down her cheek. Helena sipped her wine and felt a warmth and a lessen-
ing of apprehension. Eastleigh began to kiss her bare
shoulder, murmuring huskily, "I always thought you
glorious, Nell. But tonight you are divine! That gown
is enough to drive any man out of his senses." His
hand was caressing her throat. Sliding lower. She felt
a wave of desire, of excitement. Why, at this of all
moments, must she see a pair of wistful grey eyes?
Why must she hear a deep voice say regretfully, "...A
truly happy marriage...?" Nerves quivering, she
broke away and jumped up. "Robert, this is wrong. If
your uncle does not come soon, I must leave."

He stood at once. "Nell, I have loved you, waited
for you, such a long while. You alone have my heart,
never trample it, my darling, or I will surely die. Come
to me...most adored of all women."

He was so handsome and appealing, and to be offered such devotion from the man she had loved for
years was sweet indeed. Somehow, she was in his arms
once more, her mind spinning as he kissed and ca-
ressed her. But she was not too dizzied to hear a knock

at the outer door. Reality swept back, and the moment of weakness was done. She cried frantically, "What if that should be Cliveden? Robert, I *must* go!"

"Nonsense." He kissed her hand. "How he has frightened you! But he won't dare come here again, beloved, for I sent him off with a flea in his ear, I promise you. There's nothing to fear."

"Nothing to fear! He'd call you out! Any decent man would!"

"What stuff! He knows I'm a crack shot, he'd never face me in a duel. But—" he ran his fingertips down her cheek, smiling tenderly "—if he *should* be so reckless, you could not fail to look beautiful in black, my darling."

Helena stared at him, shocked to silence by that deadly implication.

"Now there's an interesting observation."

With a choking gasp, she whirled around.

A slim Georgian gentleman wearing a neat powdered wig swung an amber cane as he watched them. He was poised and elegant in a burgundy velvet coat, the great cuffs and pocket flaps rich with silver braid. Snowy lace gleamed at wrists and throat; his waistcoat was white satin embroidered with silver; white satin small clothes, silver embroidered hose, and shoes fastened with ruby buckles completed his costume.

"Faith, but you seem to enjoy my apartments," sneered Eastleigh. "I'll have you moving in before I know it!"

Cliveden sauntered closer, his eyes a steely glitter. "I am more likely to have you moving—out." He turned to Helena and said sternly, "I expected better of you than this, madam wife."

Suddenly, she saw him through a blur of tears, and more than anything in the world she longed to be safely back at Whisperwood. "P-Peter..." she gulped.

"Our coach is waiting," he said curtly.

Feeling unutterably shamed, unutterably wretched, she bowed her head and turned to leave.

"Then by all means, occupy it, dear old boy," said Eastleigh.

Something in his voice drew Helena's glance back to him. She gave a gasp, and stood frozen. A long steel barrel gleamed blue in the firelight. The pistol was aimed steadily at Cliveden's heart.

"Robert!" she cried shrilly. "He has no weapon! Are you mad?"

"With desire, my darling. I told you I'd deal with this dog."

"No!" Terrified, she started forward.

Cliveden's arm flashed out and she was swept behind him. "True to form, eh, Rob?" he said contemptuously. Ignoring the menace of the pistol, he stepped closer, demanding, "How did you lure my wife here?"

"Your wife—but *my* love." Eastleigh saw the murderous light in the grey eyes, and his fingers tightened around the trigger. "You've earned this, you lying cheat."

Helena knew suddenly that he meant to fire. She shrieked, "Robert, *no*!"

"Murder?" drawled Cliveden, strolling another dauntless step towards that deadly muzzle. "They'll hang you, my poor fool."

"It won't be murder," smiled Eastleigh. "I have two witnesses to testify that you attacked me. Your wife. And my man. Sorry, Peter, but you never were worth much."

Helena glanced around desperately. The only thing to hand was the wine bottle on the table. She grabbed for it.

Before she could even aim, Cliveden's cane whipped upward and in a swift lunge was thrust firmly into the muzzle of the pistol.

Eastleigh gawked at the useless weapon in his hand.

"I believe that might be called—checkmate," murmured Cliveden.

It was so fast, so very undramatic. And Robert looked so very silly, his jaw hanging open as he gazed down at the pistol with the cane stuck in the end. Helena began to giggle helplessly.

Eastleigh ground out a curse, and snatched at the cane.

Cliveden moved twice. His left hand smashed pistol and cane to one side. His right fist came up short and sharp.

Eastleigh went down hard.

Carstairs appeared in the open doorway.

Helena warned, *"Peter!"*

Dropping into a crouch, Cliveden whirled about. In that moment he looked very far from timid, and she was briefly reminded of his expression when he had sent the team flying past the stagecoach.

The valet glanced from his master's still form to Cliveden. He said with cool imperturbability, "I believe you have dropped your cane, sir."

Cliveden grinned, and retrieved his property, then unloaded the pistol and dropped it carelessly onto the stomach of its owner. Crossing to take Helena's arm, he ushered her through the door the valet held wide.

"Is there any message, sir?" enquired Carstairs.

"Mr. Leopold Savage," murmured Cliveden. "Good evening to you."

In the carriage, Helena began to tremble uncontrollably.

Cliveden said, "We have forgot your cloak, madam. I'll get it."

"No!" She grabbed for his arm, then paused in surprise.

He detached the wine bottle from her hand. "If you really like Madeira, it is not necessary that we steal it," he said, and jumped lightly from the carriage. He was back in a second, and wrapping the cloak about her.

"Peter," she began, imploringly. "I know what you heard, but did you name Savage to act as your Second? Must there be a duel?"

His fingers touched her lips. "There is no need to discuss it. Now."

Sobs were strangling her, but she was suddenly and overwhelmingly tired. Fighting that exhaustion, trying to think of what to say to him, she could not, and minutes later, she was fast asleep.

Cliveden gathered her close against him, and gently removing her wig, rested his cheek against her rumpled, fragrant hair. "I do wish," he whispered, "that

I knew which of us you meant to hit with your bottle, my wilful little wretch...."

"AND—THAT'S THE WHOLE STORY." Helena took the handkerchief Leo Savage offered, and blew her nose daintily. "And I think you unkind to laugh so."

Savage moaned, and wiped away tears. "How I should *love* to have seen Cliveden stick his cane in that pistol barrel!" He went off into whoops again. "It is worth getting up at such an ungodly hour, just to hear of it! If the tale gets about, Eastleigh will be a proper laughingstock."

Helena leaned back in the wing chair to avoid the ray of sunlight that slanted through the morning-room windows, and watched him without affection. "You were here earlier, I understand, and now you are come back. I presume you've been arranging a horrid duel."

He sighed. "None of the duels I arrange are horrid. And if they were, I'd not discuss such things with you, my naughty but irresistible Delilah."

She shrank, and put her hands over her face. "Do not! Oh—do not!"

He pulled his chair closer and leaned to pat her shoulder. "There, there. You never meant it to come to this, I am very sure."

She seized his hand and squeezed it gratefully. "Thank you, Leo, for knowing that. But I *am* responsible! And—oh, if he should be killed...." She blinked, and pressed his handkerchief to her trembling lips.

"Stuff! He'll likely wing him is all."

"But I don't *want* him to be winged! Oh, I know he has lied, and—and been dishonourable in the extreme, but he *is* my husband now."

Savage's brows lifted, then his mouth curved into his sardonic smile. "You surprise me, Nell. I'd thought your concern was for your dashing peer. No never fly into a huff. Besides, you worry for the wrong man. Eastleigh's a fair shot, but cannot hold a candle to Cliveden."

"You must be mistaken! It is Eastleigh who's the deadly one, surely?"

"Not," he drawled, "in a fair fight." He shrugged at her astounded expression. "Ask your brother. Where *is* Ross, by the way?"

"Gone with Cliveden to collect the clock and that ugly bowl I bought at the auction." Her eyes brightened. "Leo, I was never so pleased as to see Rostyn looking so well! To think he walks with only one crutch now! He vows he'll go to the altar using no more than a cane. Is it not marvellous?"

He smiled, glad to see the anxiety banished from her exquisite little face. "Marvellous. Now—tell me about this clock...."

"BE DASHED IF EVER I SAW so quaint a device," said Rostyn, making his way out of the warehouse beside Cliveden. "Would you object to letting Geraldine see it? After I speak to her papa?"

His voice shook a little on the last sentence, and Cliveden glanced quickly at him. "Nervous?"

Rostyn flushed. "Well—yes. A trifle. I have very little to offer, you know. And she's so blasted rich! I— Dash it, people might think—"

"With your record, my dear fellow, I doubt that anyone worthwhile would think anything of the sort."

Slightly out of breath Rostyn paused for a second. "You're a deuced good man. And I know damned well I've you to thank for—"

"Where the devil is my curricle?" interrupted Cliveden, shifting his grip on the two unwieldy parcels he carried, and looking up and down the almost deserted lane. "I told my groom to wait."

A shabbily dressed man came up, touching his brow respectfully. "Mr. Cliveden? I 'spect as you're looking fer yer coach, eh sir? Yer man asked of me ter tell yer one of the horses got spooked by a dog. He bolted dahn that there lane, and now yer coach wheel's stuck in the mud, sir."

Cliveden swore under his breath, and gave the man a florin. "Can you wait here for a minute, Hammond? I'd best have a look."

Rostyn nodded and watched them walk away, then followed at his necessarily slower pace.

Cliveden's guide turned into an alley some distance from the warehouse; a narrow, refuse-strewn place of sagging weather-beaten fences edging the darkly decrepit old buildings. There was no sign of the curricle.

"Jes along here a bit, sir," whined the shabby man ingratiatingly.

A little twang of warning sounded in Cliveden's mind. He paused, his eyes narrowing. It was muddy all right, but there were no wheel tracks. Halting, he grabbed his guide's arm. "What devilry are you—"

The shabby man gave a squeal and a twist and darted off. Cliveden heard the faintest sound, and whipped around. Two ruffians ran at his back, and a third was in the act of clambering over a fence to join the attack. He was unarmed, and these were no simple thieves, for despite the harsh penalty for armed robbery, the first two carried vicious-looking knives while the third gripped a long cudgel.

Cliveden retreated quickly, set down the smaller parcel containing the clock, then snatched up a splintered piece of fence-board. He'd faced heavier odds; he'd give the ruffians a good run for their money! He crouched, grimly ready for them. They came in fast, the big greasy-haired lout to the left, his scrawny grinning accomplice to the right. Cliveden took the greasy man's initial slash on Helena's bowl, and springing aside, avoided the darting knife of the grinning bully, and drove his wooden 'sword' into the dirty waistcoat. A yowl rent the air and the man doubled up. Cliveden ducked wildly, and the third man's cudgel whistled over his head. He heard Hammond shout, then the greasy lout was hacking at him again. He thrust with his board and it was longer than the knife so the greasy man jumped back, but from the corner of his eye, Cliveden saw the cudgel whizzing at him. He flung up the bowl, shield fashion. The cudgel came down with stunning force, and the bowl shattered. Cliveden reeled, and the third man gave a howl of triumph that died into a wail as Cliveden dropped the parcel and drove his right home hard.

At the mouth of the alley Rostyn came into view, hopping frantically on his crutch. "Let be, you thieving bastards!" he shouted. *"Watch! Watch!"*

The greasy lout snarled, "Jake! Scrag the cripple 'fore he brings the Runners dahn on us!"

The scrawny man, no longer grinning, began to run at Hammond.

"Ross!" shouted Cliveden. "Go!"

For that brief second his attention was diverted, and the greasy man's knife darted again. Cliveden swayed aside desperately, gasped, and fell to one knee. The thief laughed and jumped forward, triumphant. Cliveden snatched up the package of broken glass and flailed it. The knife was dashed from the greasy one's clutch and howling oaths he ran to retrieve it. Breathless, Cliveden looked up. Rostyn was struggling, but his precarious balance was not yet ready for a brawl and he fell heavily. The scrawny man swung up his knife. With all his strength, Cliveden hurled the heavy package of shattered glass. He knew a brief satisfaction as the scrawny man went down, then a violent impact sent the muddy lane and the bright sky spinning into a crazily fragmented confusion. A savage face loomed over him. The cudgel whipped down murderously. Instinctively, Cliveden threw up one arm to protect himself. From a long way off he seemed to hear an echoing shout....

CHAPTER NINE

HELENA'S HAND SHOOK as she unwound the make-
shift bandage. When he'd first come into the house,
Cliveden had thought her about to faint, and she'd
clutched at Leo Savage like someone drowning. Now,
he sat at the table in her parlour, watching the cautious movements of that gentle little hand and thinking that she must have *some* fondness for him. Last
night, when Eastleigh had meant to put a period to
him, she had snatched up the wine bottle so valiantly.
Surely, it was at Eastleigh she'd meant to heave it? But
even if that were so, it might have been only because
she'd been afraid her lover would be hanged. His arm
jerked a little.

Helena peered at him anxiously. Her other worries
were forgotten. All she could think of was that he had
been so wickedly set upon and that she must help him.
"Oh!" she said, "I am hurting you dreadfully!"

He was very pale, but he smiled at her and said that
she was most gentle. "I assure you ma'am, the cut is
of little consequence."

'Little consequence!' thought Helena. Would she
ever forget the horror of it? She and Leo had heard the
small commotion outside, followed by cries of alarm
from the servants, and had hurried into the hall in time

to see Rostyn being carried in by the groom and a footman, and Cliveden, a gory bandage wrapped around his right forearm and his face streaked with blood, coming uncertainly up the steps leaning on the arm of a sturdy member of the Watch.

Protesting that he was "perfectly all right," Rostyn had been borne to his bedchamber. Savage had sent a lackey running for the apothecary, and Mrs. Vernon had rushed to tend Rostyn.

Helena peeled away the rest of the bandage, and gave a gasp as a deep gash was revealed. She had grown up with three brothers, and the sight of blood was not unfamiliar to her, but she could not seem to stop shaking, and had to fight an almost overwhelming need to burst into tears.

Emma came in with a tray of medical supplies and a steaming brass ewer. She gave a small squeal when she caught a glimpse of Cliveden's arm, and fled gladly when Helena sent her to find out how Mr. Hammond went on.

"Ross isn't too badly damaged," said Cliveden, quick to note the tremor in his wife's voice.

"Ar, thanks to you, sir," put in the Watchman, who hovered nearby clutching the stub of a pencil and a grubby notebook. "Had you not throwed that there parcel, the other gent would've been—"

"And had you not been to hand so promptly, I think I'd have gone with him. I'm obliged to you, friend."

Basking in the glow of the gentleman's very pleasant smile, and the happy recipient of a more substantial token of thanks, the Watchman said that he'd spotted a couple of ugly customers loitering about the vicinity earlier in the day. "But then they sorta drifted orf like. Just the same, I was on the cue veevey, like the Frenchies say, and I come on the run when I heard Mr. Hammond shouting."

"Were they common thieves then?" asked Helena, beginning with extreme caution to bathe the injury.

"That they was not, marm," replied the Watchman importantly. "Not your simple buzzmen or foot scamperers, marm. Capital was their lay, no doubting. And it'll be Newgate and the nubbing cheat, if I gets these here hands on 'em! As I will, marm. A grand fight your husband put up, marm, else his friend would've—"

Cliveden, who had been rendered rather short of breath, now recovered his voice and advised the Watchman that he talked too much. "It was a simple matter of thieves who knew that valuables would be carried out of the warehouse. The worst aspect of the business," he added, turning to Helena, "is that the rogues got my mama's clock!"

The apothecary arrived at this point, and both Helena and the Watchman were banished. They went together to Hammond's room. Rostyn was laid down upon his bed, with Daniels keeping watch beside him, Mrs. Vernon having gone down to the kitchen to brew a posset. Helena was vastly relieved to discover that her brother was more shaken than hurt, his most serious injury being a vivid bruise across his ribs, where he'd been kicked when he tried to struggle to his feet. His crutch had been smashed during the battle, but he told Helena cheerfully that fortunately Daniels had brought both crutches from Sussex, so this was a small loss. "Poor Cliveden took the worst of it."

"Right you are, sir," said the Watchman, who'd been writing in his little notebook. "The perishers meant to do fer him, they did. Ar, and would've if I hadn't gone and got my pop after I see them varmints s'morning!"

Helena's enquiry elicited the information that one of the thieves had been shot and was dead, but the other two had escaped with the clock. She was appalled to think that a man had lost his life in the commission of the crime, but more appalled by the knowledge that they had meant to kill her husband.

"Likely they didn't want Mr. Cliveden alive to point 'em out," said the Watchman, and closing his notebook went "back on duty."

Helena stayed with Rostyn for a short while, then returned to her parlour to find that Cliveden had been packed off to his bed. The apothecary was just closing the door when she reached his room and was adamant in denying her admission. Mr. Savage, he said, was "tiring" his patient at the moment, but had been warned to stay only a very short time.

She walked down the stairs with him, demanding to know just how serious were her husband's injuries. "For a man of his stamp, nothing to mention, ma'am," he responded cheerfully. "The wound in the arm is relatively minor, but he took a nasty rap from that cudgel and I'd prefer he was resting. However, he would have his way, so—" he shrugged, and said dryly that he presumed Mr. Savage was a close friend.

Helena confirmed this. "I really don't know what I would have done had he not been with me when the curricle came back," she said tremulously.

The apothecary clicked his tongue. The poor young lady looked ready to swoon, which was not to be wondered at. "A terrible shock for you," he said sympathetically, and deplored the crime that was allowed to run rampant on London's streets. Then, having advised Helena that her husband must be kept quiet, and that the wounded arm should be carried in a sling for a day or two, he took himself to the kitchen to accept Mrs. Vernon's offer of a cup of tea.

Helena wandered into the withdrawing room and waited anxiously for Savage to come downstairs. She felt cold and frightened and wished her mother was at home. Mrs. Hammond had gone to a meeting to endorse Lord Erskine's efforts to prevent cruelty to animals, and to discuss the formation of a society to further his ideals. Helena doubted she would return until late afternoon, and she felt tearful and unwilling to be alone. She would have gone up to be with Rostyn again, save that she meant to talk with Savage before he departed, and suspected he would try to leave without seeing her.

Her suspicions were confirmed ten minutes later, when she heard soft voices in the hall, and caught him, hat in hand, in the act of slipping out of the front door. She brushed aside his feeble excuses and bore him into the breakfast parlour where an appetizing luncheon had been set out. Savage sighed, said that he knew when he was outmanoeuvred, and joined her at the table, but groaned when Helena dismissed the servants.

"Now, Nell, there's no use putting me through an inquisition. Cliveden has the headache but seems little the worse for his small war. As for the rest, you may be sure he wasn't about to speak of—ahem, personal matters."

"No, of course, but I can guess what you did discuss."

"Nothing for a lady's ears." He shook a chicken wing at her. "You must not ask me about it. Talk to Cliveden yourself. Thanks to my unprecedented stupidity you're his wife, not mine."

She sighed miserably. "I've not had a moment alone with him since last night. Besides, he shares your silly notions that the ladies must not be told about such horrid events as duels. He's very good at—at trickery." She thought of how he had 'tricked' Rostyn back to health, and cried imploringly, "Oh, Leo, *must* there be a duel?"

"My dear lady! Eastleigh was ready to blow Cliveden's head off, and Cliveden not only made him look very foolish, but then proceeded to knock him down! Surely you see that a duel is quite unavoidable?"

She gave an impatient gesture. "No matter what you say, he cannot fire a pistol with that hurt arm. The duel must be postponed."

Savage helped himself to another piece of chicken and said blandly, "Couldn't agree more."

"Thank heaven! Then you will go and explain to Lord Eastleigh?"

"Cliveden has hordes of friends," he grumbled. "I wish he'd not chosen me for his second. Oh, I know I'm soon to be part of the family, and he wants this kept quiet as possible, but it's a pestiferous business." He paused, then added, "Unless they both shoot very straight. In which case—would you have me, fair one?"

Helena felt a pang of terror, but he was joking, of course. She replied with a rueful smile, "Are you very sure you would still want me for a wife?"

Suddenly, his eyes were quite without mockery. "If ever you find yourself sans spouse, my dear, I will prove how much I want you."

He left at three o'clock, saying he would go and break the news of the attack to his sister, before trying to find Eastleigh. Half an hour later a frightened Geraldine had arrived from their family home on Grosvenor Place. Helena took her straight up to her brother's room. Rostyn was awake and talking with his man. The joy that lit his face when he saw his beloved touched Helena's heart, and she defied convention by leaving them alone.

The minutes dragged past. By half past four she was running to the windows of the library each time she heard carriage wheels, but Savage still had not returned when Mrs. Hammond came home at a quarter to five, and the story had to be told all over again.

Geraldine stayed to dinner. Helena's obvious nervousness was attributed to the terrible events of the day, and she was urged to go early to bed. On the way she looked in on Cliveden. She felt shy to see him lying in the great bed looking rumpled and youthful. Fulton, his balding and somewhat dour valet, said gruffly that the apothecary had left a draught to make the master sleep and he would probably not awaken until morning.

For Helena, sleep was out of the question. Frantic because Savage had not returned, and unable to share her fears with anyone, she paced back and forth in her little parlour. Why did he not come? And when was the duel to be fought? Tomorrow, perhaps? The knife wound in Cliveden's forearm had required stitching. It would be stiff and painful, reducing his chances. But Robert was a sportsman to the core. He'd never insist upon so unfair an advantage.

Emma came and went, watching her anxiously, and when Helena sank into a chair at length, a hand over her eyes, the abigail ran to kneel beside her. "Oh, ma'am, you've worried half the night away! I cannot bear to see you so upset! Is it because of Mr. Cliveden and your poor brother?"

Shocked by her own thoughtlessness, Helena apologized for not having sent the abigail to her bed hours since, but Emma would not leave her in what she termed "a proper state." Helena yielded to the temptation to talk to someone about her troubles, and confided that Mr. Savage was to have brought her a most important message. "He did not come, and I am concerned lest something may be wrong."

The girl beamed with relief. "Mr. Savage did bring something this afternoon, ma'am. He said I wasn't to give it to you 'til morning, but—"

"This *afternoon*?" Helena sprang to her feet. "Show me."

Emma hesitated, then reached into her apron pocket and took out a letter.

With a little cry of exasperation, Helena snatched it from her hand and broke the seals. The writing was typical of Savage, a lazy scrawl, difficult to read.

"Fairest,
  You are the loveliest lady in all England, and gladly would I fight for you, kill for you, die for you.
  But, alas, I cannot fight the Code of Honour, and Cliveden is a most stubborn fellow and refuses to ask for a postponement.
  You will recall I did not actually say I would approach Eastleigh in the matter.
  I am a sly man, and a coward. I own it.
                    Forgive your ever adoring,
                                    Savage

THERE WAS A DRIZZLE in the air and the night was very dark when the fashionable chariot stopped outside the tall house on Ryder Street. Helena pulled her hood closer, and took the hand her personal footman extended. Stepping down onto the wet flagway, she whispered, "What is the time, Herbert?"

"Twenty minutes past three o'clock, ma'am." Herbert was a married man, and he glanced unhappily at the flambeaux which blazed on either side of the front door. Lord Eastleigh might have guests, and they might not be the kind this very delightful young lady should meet. "Mrs. Cliveden," he ventured cautiously, "are you quite sure you wouldn't rather wait 'til morning?"

Grateful for that concern, Helena captivated him with her smile and said she was very sure. "If the coachman must walk the horses, please do you wait here for me."

Herbert nodded and when the porter had responded to his knock, took up his station at the front step, grimly resolved to guard his beautiful mistress against all Marshall Ney's famous cavalry if the need arose.

Carstairs betrayed none of the thinly veiled scorn the porter had evidenced upon admitting a young lady of quality to a gentleman's flat at this hour of the morning. The master was out, said the valet with his customary urbanity, but was expected momentarily. "Does madam desire to wait?"

Praying the wait would not be a long one, Helena indicated that such was her desire. She was ushered into the parlour. Carstairs lit a branch of candles, offered refreshments, and these being refused, bowed and departed, an odd little smile lurking about the corners of his mouth.

Helena sat on a blue satin chair and stared at the glowing candles as the clock ticked the time away. Robert must be at a party. If it was a card party, he might not come home until dawn. But if he was out this late, the duel certainly could not be scheduled for tomorrow morning—or for *this* morning, rather. That was a relief, at least. If Peter learned she had been here again...! She bit her lip. Still, it was for his sake she was here. Robert loved her devotedly; he would do anything she asked. The clock ticked on, and her thoughts churned and her nervousness grew. Tick tock, tick tock... She seemed to have spent most of this hideous day waiting for one gentleman or another. When would he *come*? Her restless glance flitted about the room. Tick tock, tick tock... A charming room, as she'd noticed the last time. Elegant furnishings...fine prints... And—no clock. She thought curiously, 'How odd! I'd have sworn...' Tilting her head, she could hear it distinctly. A clock *was* ticking, and it was in this room. Why ever could she not see it?

The chime that sounded the half-hour was daintily melodious, but it might have been a thunderclap. Helena uttered an involuntary cry, and every vestige of colour left her face. Her eyes opened very wide and saw only Peter, laughter lurking in his grey eyes as he said, "Ever the practical female... The dial is just below the middle mast...."

Trembling, she began to wander about the room, following the sound of the ticking. It led to the credenza which stood against the rear wall. She opened the door and whispered an anguished, "Oh—*no*! My God! Oh, my God!"

Watching through the slightly open door, Carstairs heard the sobbed out words, saw the dainty figure crumple, the proud little head bow into two clutching hands. His smile broadened and became vindictively triumphant, and smiling still, he crept away.

Soon afterwards, a lady with hood pulled low over her face left the house on Ryder Street, a bulky object clutched under her cloak. The waiting footman sprang eagerly to usher her into the chariot; the coachman's whip cracked, and the luxurious vehicle lurched and rolled smoothly away.

Ryder Street was quiet again, only the stamp of an impatient hoof betraying the presence of another coach farther up the street and all but invisible in the deeper shadow of a tree. One of the occupants sighed wearily, leaned back against the squabs and closed his eyes. The other man swore and said an irritated, "I told you not to follow her!"

Cliveden scarcely heard. "I didn't really...believe," he muttered to himself. "But, when she thought me in a drugged sleep, she ran to...him."

There was a note in the deep voice that made even so hardened a rake as Leopold Savage wince. "What a damnable bumble broth you put me in," he grumbled. But added in a kinder tone, "Don't be a fool, man. Let me take you home. You're in no condition to fight. I'll explain to Eastleigh. He won't dare object in front of the seconds."

Cliveden whispered dully, "He gave her something, did you see? She held something. A gift for my dear wife, before he..." The words faded.

"Dammit!" Savage rapped on the roof. "We're going to my rooms! Coachman—"

"By God, but we're not!" Recovering his aplomb, Cliveden jerked upright and called in a voice that brooked no argument. "To Wimbledon, John Coachman. And be very sure we are not one minute late!"

THE JOURNEY BACK TO Cliveden House was accompanied by a sudden downpour, but it might have been bright sunshine for all Helena saw of it. Her eyes were blank and tearless, and in her cold hands the little galleon clock ticked faithfully but unheard. There could be only one logical answer for Robert to have the clock. He must have master-minded the attack. He'd known when Peter meant to go to the warehouse, for she herself had given him the information. But—why? Why should the gallant young man she had worshipped for so many years devise a scheme which was against every concept he had been bred up to respect; contrary to every law of fair play and decency?

She shivered, and against her will, many little instances that had troubled her began to creep into her mind. Robert's carelessness about the rights of others; his sneeringly disparaging remarks about Peter; the somehow unconvincing explanation for his having failed to seek her out upon his return to England; his often less than polite language while in the presence of ladies; the arrogant way he'd dragged her from that crowded ballroom, not caring how she was humiliated nor who was jostled. Trite things, perhaps, but taken together they painted an unpleasant picture. Had he cared that Peter might have been killed in the robbery? Her beloved brother had also been set upon by those brutal thieves!

The door was swung open, and she blinked at Herbert.

"We've a caller, by the look of things, ma'am," he murmured.

She thought, 'At this hour?' but when she alighted saw a large coach drawn up before her own. She caught a glimpse of a crest on the panel, then was hurrying up the steps.

In the entrance hall the tall figure of Viscount Burtonbrook faced Chartley and a scared footman. The butler, who had always seemed distinguished but pompous, now looked like a distracted and kindly grandfather, his dressing gown loosely tied, revealing a garish red-and-white nightshirt. Seeing Helena come in, he tugged the dressing gown closed while proclaiming in a worried manner that the master was "already gone."

Helena's breath was snatched away and she stood rigid and very cold.

"Gone?" His lordship's anger was resonant. "Where, pray?"

Helena pulled her scattered wits together, "I believe I know, my lord." They all turned to her, and ignoring their obvious astonishment, she handed the clock to the footman and went on, "My husband is to fight a duel with your nephew. I presume that is why you are come."

He put up his quizzing glass and scanned her. "Ah, yes. The young Mrs. Cliveden—who almost was Lady Robert Eastleigh." His lip curled. He said bitterly, "You had a narrow escape, madam."

She flushed. "I begin to suspect you are correct, my lord. Of more immediate importance, however, you should know that Cliveden has hurt his right arm. The duel must be stopped."

"I fancy that I know the cause of this duel. Which being the case, unless I mistake him, Cliveden would fight had he no arms at all!"

His eyes seemed to pierce her, and it was all Helena could do to meet them. She tried to speak, but he lifted one hand regally, and turned to Chartley. "Mr. Rostyn Hammond is far from well, I know, so I'll not ask that you disturb him. Conduct me to Mr. Cliveden's valet. At once, man!"

Chartley threw a frightened glance at Helena, then led the viscount up the stairs. Helena turned and slipped quietly away.

FOR A LONG TIME the silence in the great carriage was broken only by the rumble of wheels and the rhythmic beat of sixteen polished hooves. Then, Lord Burtonbrook said in a kinder voice than he had used thus far, "Mrs. Cliveden, I must believe that what you've told me is truth, wherefore you have my deepest sympathy. Nonetheless, you had no business to slip uninvited into my coach, and have less business insisting upon accompanying me to what may well be a very ugly confrontation."

"If it is so, my lord," she said steadily, "the fault is mine. But if we are in time, I know Robert will listen to me, and this tragedy can be averted."

"Would that I might share your optimism, ma'am. And—forgive the contradiction—the fault is not yours. If anyone is at fault in this particular contretemps—I am that person."

Helena stared at his hawklike profile, outlined against the faintly brightening eastern skies. "But—" she said uncertainly, "how are you involved, sir?"

"From long and long ago." For a moment, he hesitated, as if doing battle with himself. Then he went on, "Robert was the only son of my favourite sister, and the most handsome, delightful little boy. But very soon, even the most doting of us came to see that he was wilful and selfish. At Eton he acquired a reputation for wildness. The older he became, the more outrageous the escapades." He sighed broodingly, then continued, "General Sir Ian Cliveden is one of my dearest friends and his son Peter was at school with Robert. I'd hoped they would become friends also, but Robert despised Peter, making the mistake so many people make, and confusing gentleness with weakness. Peter was not above his own share of mischief, but he was manly and straightforward, and never tried to escape responsibility for what he'd done. Unconsciously perhaps, I began to hold him up to Robert as the example of what an honourable young fellow should be. That was disastrous, of course. A year or so ago, Robert got himself into a particularly ugly business. I was able to keep it quiet, and I bought him a pair of colours. It didn't serve. He was soon in trouble for—oh, many things. I drafted a new will disinheriting him. Then, I discovered he admired you. I could not have been more pleased. I've known your Mama for years in a remote way, and I'd kept an eye on you and your brothers. Your lineage is beyond reproach, and I thought you could be the making of the boy. I told him I would restore his inheritance on the day he married you. Then..." He shrugged. "Spain. And— Pity. Great pity."

The scales were dropping rapidly from Helena's eyes. She felt humiliated and angry, and asked, "Why did you not tell me he'd been wounded? Why did you allow me to marry Cliveden, believing Robert killed? That was cruel, sir!"

"And you despised Cliveden, I don't doubt, for lying to you!" He gave a harsh bark of laughter. "Y'know m'dear, this great city never ceases to amaze me. Gossip, slander, viciousness, sweep the ton like a flame, and everyone knows of the latest *affaire de coeur* almost before it has become a fait accompli. Yet some things are kept as close as a bishop's purse! All London knew what happened at Badajoz. All except Mistress Helena Hammond, apparently!"

"I know now that Robert was wounded and—"

"Tush and a fiddlestick! He was not so much as scratched! While countless gallant young men were sacrificing their lives for their country; while your fine brother was getting himself blown up, and your despised husband was one of the first to be shot off the scaling ladders—*my* noble kinsman was—running, Mrs. Cliveden! Lord Robert Haitland Eastleigh," his voice shook a little, "deserted his men and...ran from the action!"

Helena gave a gasp of horror, but could think of nothing to say. After a brief and rather terrible silence, the viscount went on harshly, "Now can you wonder that I left Town so suddenly? That I could not bear to reveal our shame to you? Can you see why young Cliveden told you Robert was dead? To the ton he *is* dead. Worse than dead! He was asked to resign his commission, and is damned lucky he was not executed on the spot! However, the facts are out now, and he is ostracized, ma'am. Shunned. He has received not one invitation since he came home."

"But—I first met him again at a party! And he was at the Wansford masquerade ball."

He gave a snort of disgust. "If he was at any party, he entered by the back door, and likely left by the same route. I suppose he'd be fairly safe at a masked ball. But in neither instance was he an invited guest, I promise you! Cliveden knew the life you would lead if you married my nephew. He may have lied so as to win you himself, but he also lied to spare you. You should go down on your knees and thank God for that lie, young lady!"

Through her own remorse, Helena could feel this proud old gentleman's heartbreak. Without a word, she reached out and put her hand over his. After a second, she heard a muffled grunt, then his hand turned and gripped her own tightly. She said, her voice uneven, "Whatever will become of him?"

His grip became crushing. "He is an expensive young rascal and I have cut him down to what he would term a pittance. I told him he could live well on it in the colonies, and that he must leave England." He grunted sardonically. "My fine grand-nephew informed me that he has no intention of leaving England. I'll not mince words, he is mad for you. But he also wants a rich wife."

Helena closed her eyes briefly. "So—that is why he didn't come and find me when he came home from

Spain. I was poverty stricken." She frowned suddenly. "But—why pursue me now?"

She heard the viscount draw a breath. He said harshly, "Cliveden ain't poverty stricken."

Her mind could not at once unravel this; then she cried, appalled, "The—the duel? And—then he means to court me? No! Oh, no! I cannot believe that of him!"

"No more you should. Robert's not a fool. If he kills Peter in a duel, he'll have to fly the country, and it would be more than you'd dare do—however infatuated you are—to marry the man who made you a widow!"

'However infatuated you are.' Shivering, she asked, "Then, what . . . ?"

He said reluctantly, "Heaven help me, it is my belief that the attack on your husband yesterday was only made to seem a theft. The real object was to kill Cliveden. Before the duel. Robert would then appear blameless."

After a moment, Helena said huskily, "Was there ever such a fool as I have been? Thank heaven it has ended like this. Instead of—"

"It ain't over yet, m'dear," the viscount interposed dryly.

Her gaze flew to him. "But you said Robert wouldn't fight!"

"Not while there was a chance he could get others to do his dirty work for him. But even Robert knows when he's at Point Non-Plus. If he hopes to find another—ah—if he hopes to win a rich bride, he must retain some vestige of a reputation. He'll fight. But it

won't be the easy win he imagined. He chose to regard your husband as a spineless coward. Only recently has he learned that Cliveden is a fine fighting
man and an excellent shot. Cool, steady, deadly. A
formidable opponent.''

"Thank God," whispered Helena. "He will have a
chance, then.''

The Viscount said no more, unwilling to put his
deepest fear into words. The fear that when a weak
man's back is to the wall there's no telling what he may
do.

SIR EVERARD PAYNTON, Cliveden's favourite cousin,
strode across the dewy grass with a dark scowl on his
pleasant face. Savage, examining the case of duelling
pistols, asked with a sneer, "Think they'll bring their
man up to snuff?''

"Not much doubt of that. The beastly fellow's
boasting of just where he means to place his shot!''
Paynton glanced at Cliveden who sat against a nearby
tree poking his cane absently at the damp soil. Lowering his voice, he said, "And he damned well might
do it! Peter's a fool not to have postponed. He can
scarce use that arm. Did you see him when I handed
him my own pistol? He almost dropped it!''

Cliveden, who possessed extremely acute hearing
said, "Stop moaning, Pay. I'll shoot, I promise you.''

There was an unfamiliar harshness in his voice, and
his cousin exclaimed in alarm, "Not to kill, dear old
boy? Don't want to have to trot out of the country.
Awful disappointment for my dear aunt.''

Cliveden made no response but continued to prod at the earth, testing his arm. It was painfully stiff, but he'd hold the pistol up somehow. 'Not to kill...?' His jaw set. Mama would understand. And much Paynton knew of it. Eastleigh wanted killing—the sooner the better!

They were ready. Savage gave him a hand up, and Paynton helped him button his coat so as to shut out as much of the white shirt as possible.

They walked to the site. Eastleigh stood there looking like some Greek hero, head thrown up proudly, an expression of lofty disdain on his handsome, if sweat streaked face. Cliveden regarded him grimly, but Eastleigh would not meet his eyes. Probably ashamed to do so, the filthy sneaking hound. And Helena, his exquisite little reluctant wife had gone to this man last night. Again...she had gone to him....

"Choose your weapons, gentlemen."

Eastleigh took up a weapon. Well aware that the man watched his hand intently, Cliveden closed his fingers around the butt of the remaining long and deadly duelling pistol. He'd never before noticed how big they were. And Lord, but it was heavy! He began to sweat himself, but forced his arm to take the weight and struggled to keep his face impassive. He walked to his appointed place. The sun was coming up. It was such a beautiful morning. And life could have been so beautiful. With her. Only she wanted this pretty bastard. 'Helena—couldn't you have loved me? Just a little? I love you so very much, my Helena....'

"Stand ready, gentlemen...."

Gritting his teeth, he lifted the pistol to the approved position, the barrel pointing at the brightening skies.

Paynton shouted for a delay and walked over to him. What the hell was he doing?

"Peter," said his cousin urgently. "You look like the very deuce. For the love of God, let me ask for a postponement."

"Pay, be so good as to go to the devil!" But the distress in the honest face broke through his own misery. He said softly, "Have you looked at Eastleigh? He's one large twitch. Chin up, old lad."

Paynton gave him a rather crooked smile and retreated.

Wondering for how many more seconds he could hold up this brutally heavy pistol, Cliveden saw Helena in the garden, holding First Cat, her lovely face alight with laughter as the animal sagged lazily in her hands...

"Be ready, gentlemen...."

...Saw her looking at him with a smile curving her vivid lips.

"At the count of three...."

...Saw her kneeling on the bed with her head sticking through the curtains, and later lying there with fear in her eyes and that delicious nightdress revealing so much of her beautiful body.

"One..."

If he killed this bastard, would it break her dear heart? He wouldn't—

"Two..."

A mighty hand smashed the air from his lungs and sent him hurtling back.

Shouts of rageful accusation and horror. A shrill terrible screaming. Helena! Inexplicably, he was lying in the wet grass. Boots were running to him. He was tired...so tired... But he must see her.... He *must*...! Panting, he dragged himself onto one elbow. Helena was running across the clearing. Eastleigh ran to meet her, and pulled her into his arms.

Peter Cliveden groaned, fell back and lay very still.

CHAPTER TEN

HELENA RAN WILDLY ALONG the hall, her dressing gown flying out behind her, the occasional broad candles flickering as she passed them, the footman thudding along after her. Through these four terrible days and nights she had become accustomed to such rude awakenings, for it seemed as if each time she snatched a few minutes of sleep, she no sooner lay down than they had to come for her.

She could hear Peter before she reached his room. A nurse was waiting at the door and flung it wide, relief coming into her anxious face. Cliveden was sitting up in bed, struggling furiously against his valet and the other nurses who were striving to hold him down. His hollowed eyes glittering with fever, he was reliving the assault on Badajoz, shouting to his men to follow him, and already starting to cough painfully. Helena flew to stroke his flushed cheek and beg him to rest. "You must lie down, Peter," she urged, praying this attack had not caused another haemorrhage. "Come dear—lie back, please. For my sake."

Gradually he quieted, and at last they were able to lower him carefully. The burst of strength had gone. He was limp and spent, his voice a thread when he gasped out, "Helena...my Helena...where are you?"

It was a familiar cry, and as usual, her heart was wrung. She stroked the tumbled hair from his burning forehead, and bent to kiss him. "I am here, my darling. Close beside you. Try to sleep, dearest. Quiet, now...."

The nurse hurried forward and unbuttoned Cliveden's nightshirt, checking the thick bandages wrapped so tightly about his chest. The linen was blessedly unstained, and Helena gave a gasping sob of relief.

Fulton, who had served Cliveden for twelve years, and scolded and bullied and was devoted to him, murmured softly, "Thank God! If only we could keep him quiet, he'd have a better chance."

"We shall," said Helena. "I'll stay."

The nurses looked at each other worriedly.

Fulton argued, "But—ma'am, you're fair worn out. You *must* get some rest."

"Then fetch me a couch and some bedding. I'll sleep in here so that I can be at hand when the delirium takes him." She saw anxiety in their faces, but although she ached with weariness, would not be persuaded to return to her own soft bed. She knew beyond all doubting that Peter had small wish to live, and if he died—she would have killed him. "Please do not argue," she said with quiet determination. "I will not leave my husband again."

THE SPIDER WAS THERE AGAIN today. Cliveden watched it drowsily. It was a very small spider that dwelt in one corner of the canopy of his bed, and it was most industrious, always bustling about in its small home. He wondered idly if it was lonely, living in such solitude. So small a creature in so large a world. Did spiders get lonely? People got lonely. He frowned. Why was he lying here in bed when it was very obviously morning? He pushed back the blankets and gave a small shocked cry.

Many people were hovering over him, and talking in low voices, only he couldn't see their faces clearly. Someone said, "He's awake! Praise God!" Cliveden thought he would much rather still be asleep. Another kindly voice said, "He is in much pain." And Mrs. Vernon's voice urgently, "Wake the mistress. Quick!"

He whispered feebly, "No."

A gentle hand was bathing his face. Mrs. Vernon said, "He's delirious again. Never heed him."

"*No!* Keep her away! I don't want...to see her! I *won't*...see her!" Only now they couldn't seem to hear him, and the pain was so bad that everything became blurred and far away and eventually disappeared altogether.

IT WAS AMAZING, thought Helena, watching Chartley usher out the latest callers, how many people were Peter's friends. He had kept her so shut away from Town and Society that she'd had no idea she had married one of the most popular young men in London. From the moment that word of the duel had become public knowledge, they'd come. Streams of them. Fond relations, dashing young officers; elegant men about town with their equally elegant wives; distinguished wits and scholars; and some shy-eyed members of the rank and file who had served under "the Lieutenant" and held him in such high regard they had braved the imposing entrance of Cliveden House so as to make their enquiries. All asking anxiously for the latest word of his condition. And if Helena saw a trace of censure in the eyes of some of the ladies, she could not blame them, for rumour had spread its wings, and she could well imagine what the gossips had made of the ugly affair. Actually, she saw only a small percentage of those who came, for she was usually in the sick room. To her mother and Rostyn fell the duty of receiving the flowers and fruit, of relaying the news that Mr. Cliveden was doing a little better today, and of extending the family's thanks for the expressions of sympathy and affection.

Every day the florist's cart came with bouquets large and small, and every day there was a single bunch of violets and a blank card whereon was written the single letter "D." When Helena first saw the flowers, she looked at the card curiously. It took a few minutes for her to remember that Eastleigh had said Cliveden's mistress's name was Dorothy. She never displayed the slightest interest in the violets after that, but they haunted her dreams.

"DEAR LADY," said Dr. Turnbull, bustling into the withdrawing room and eyeing Helena askance, "you are very tired."

"We are all tired," she said quietly, taking the hand he extended and enduring the crushing grip that was typical of this small, fierce gentleman.

He hurled his rotund form into the chair she indicated, then regarded her searchingly. "These past
three weeks have been a nightmare for you."

"For my husband especially."

"Yes, yes, poor fellow. Dreadful business. Dreadful. But that is why we have the nurses, dear lady. You
have worn yourself to a shade, when you should have
let *them* do all the work."

Helena stood and walked over to the window. The
August afternoon was quite warm. Delilah was chasing a grasshopper in the garden. "Thank you for your
concern," she said, and returning, stood before him
and asked gravely, "Is that why you asked to see me,
doctor?"

He stared at her. He still found it incredible that a
lady who was so angelically lovely, who had fought
with such ferocity for the life of a man who wanted
only to lose it, could also be a faithless wanton. He
came to his feet and cleared his throat. "Cliveden's
considerably improved," he said. "And—well, we
have to aah—humph, think of you now." His laugh
was a little forced. "Can't have you falling ill, Mrs.
Cliveden. You must get out. Go shopping, as you ladies love to do. Or pop down to Brighton—I hear the
town grows by leaps and bounds, and the Regent's
Marine Pavilion is to be expanded and made even
more splendid. A change of air will do you the world
of good."

Helena's heart sank, but she met his eyes unwaveringly. "Sir, you need not tiptoe about. You have heard
all the gossip, I am very sure, and you have heard my

dear husband's delirious outcries. Are you asking me
to go away?''

He had not expected such forthrightness. Running
a chubby finger around the top of his neckcloth, he
stammered, ''Ah—good gracious, ma'am, I—''

''Has Mr. Cliveden asked that I no longer care for
him?''

The little doctor coughed, gestured helplessly, and
finally said a miserable, ''He is still a very sick man,
you understand. And—and anything which distresses
him compounds the aah—humph risks, d'ye see?''

Helena turned away. She felt drowned in tears, and
fighting for control, thought, 'You have only yourself to blame, you foolish girl!' With an effort which
racked her, she said, ''I quite understand. My husband shall convalesce without my...disastrous presence.'' She turned back, smiling bravely.

Dr. Turnbull shook her hand with considerably less
ferocity, averted his glance from her tear-wet eyes and
''aah—humphed'' his way from the room.

LYING ON THE CHAISE LONGUE before the windows of
the withdrawing room, Cliveden gazed fixedly into the
summer afternoon. ''I have instructed my solicitors to
make ample provision for you,'' he said. ''I shall remove to Sussex, but this house will be at your disposal for so long as you wish.''

Helena was very quiet, and he risked a quick glance
at her. She would have to wear that particular gown.
The soft peach colour made her skin appear almost
translucent. She had changed a little, he thought. She
looked more the poised young woman, and less the

glowing girl who had stolen his heart when first he'd seen her coming down the stairs of the little house off Fitzroy Square. He had put the sorrow in her glorious dark eyes and caused that tender mouth to droop. And in return she had stayed by him, nursed him, saved his life, beyond doubting. Whatever the cost, he could no longer bind her to a contract that was hateful to her.

Helena said in an odd little voice, "Are you sure it is safe for you to drive so far, Peter?"

"Oh yes. I am nearly well now. And I must thank you for all your care of me." His smile was blinding. "I know I was a great nuisance."

"Are you . . . going to give me a . . . divorce, then?"

"Beastly nuisance, isn't it? But at least it offers us a way out. You have wanted it, and I've come to want it also. I must put my life in order again. I made rather a muddle of things. I'm sorry for that, and I wish you every happiness in your future—er, future."

He was taking care not to look at her now, and Helena was able to watch the sunlight glinting on his fair hair. It had grown rather long and shaggy during his illness, and showed a decided tendency to curl, which she found devastatingly attractive. He was so cool, so self-assured. How could she dare plead with him? How beg him for another chance? Yet, she heard herself say, "I know you were reluctant to upset General Cliveden and your mama. If there is a difficulty, I—"

"No, no. My father is a good old boy and will understand. And I'm sure my solicitors will handle the business as discreetly as is possible."

"I see. And—and what shall you do, Peter?" She blushed, and said in confusion, "Not that I've the right to ask."

"Of course you've a right. You've always known that I am deeply attached to a—a certain lady. So I've decided to throw convention to the wind."

Another turn of the knife under her ribs. "You are to be married?"

"Yes. I hope you will wish me happy."

"I do. She is a very lucky lady. When do you plan to leave?"

"Tomorrow morning. I will have your things sent here, if that would be convenient?"

He wanted all traces of her out of his sight quickly. And who could blame him? Dear heaven, who could blame him? Almost, her folly had cost him his life! She said something—heaven knows what. Something polite and inane and stupid, when she longed to say "I love you! I *love* you! Forgive me!" But one did not say such things under these circumstances. She heard herself saying instead the ghastly words, "Goodbye, Peter." And she left him.

Watching the door close, Cliveden's thin hand tightened its death grip on the blanket which Fulton had insisted must cover him, even though it was a very warm afternoon. She was gone, and all that was left him was a hint of that faint sweet scent she used. What a hopeless fool, that he still loved her, knowing she could scarcely wait to leave him. She'd almost run, she was so eager to go to Eastleigh. It didn't matter evidently, that her beloved had behaved with such total dishonour; that he was a coward and a blackguard.

She loved him just the same; and who could tell why a good woman would love a worthless rogue?

Tomorrow he would go back to the serene tranquillity of Whisperwood, where he could perhaps regain some peace of mind while his body healed. A small voice jeered that he could not escape the pain of loss that was so much worse than physical pain; that he was hiding himself away, as a hurt animal seeks solitude while it licks its wounds. But he knew he could take no more. And he had his memories, at least. At the height of the fever it had been difficult to distinguish dreams from reality, but he seemed to remember Helena bending over him, her great dark eyes tearful with sympathy. He was almost sure that often he'd heard her speaking to him with ineffable compassion; had he dreamed she'd touched his hair, his cheek, with her cool caressing fingers? And, most precious of all—only this had certainly been a dream—the moment when she had said so tenderly, "My darling...."

TWO WEEKS LATER, Cliveden yawned, stretched, and turned in the big bed to face his companion. The bedcurtains were not closed, and morning sunlight angled through the windows waking a bright sheen on her golden head and lighting her drowsy blue eyes. She blinked at him seductively.

"You are excessive charming, m'dear," he said, running a caressing hand down her silken shoulder. "I am more than grateful for the nights you have spent with me. But—enough is enough. There is room on my bed for you and me, but when you bring in your children, by Gad ma'am, it is too much."

The female thus chastised demonstrated her lack of proper manners by rolling over on her back and showing him her stomach. Cliveden promptly advised her that she wanted for conduct, and returned to her the two kittens who were staggering near-sightedly about the eiderdown in search of sustenance.

A low laugh sent his gaze flashing to the doorway. Rostyn Hammond stood there, fully dressed, leaning on his cane. "Slugabed," he said, grinning. "There's another of The Mushroom's brood halfway under your pillow."

Cliveden retrieved the culprit. "Ring for my man, there's a good fellow. And take these potential clients away before they commandeer my breakfast."

Obliging, Hammond carried mother and children to the door and bestowed them on a footman. Returning to perch on the side of the bed, he pretended not to notice the dainty orange slipper on the bedside table, and observed, "You're looking almost alive again. The rural life agrees with you."

"Town life would seem to agree with you." Cliveden dropped yesterday's *Morning Chronicle* over the slipper he had stolen from his beloved, and asked casually, "When are the rites?"

"Three weeks from tomorrow. Since Kayne can't come home, Savage is going to be my best man. I'd have asked you, but I thought—" Hammond bit his lip. "Anyway, we mean to drag you there—whether or not you wish to come."

Avoiding his penetrating gaze through the following silence, Cliveden asked at length, "Has she left town yet? No, I don't mean that. I mean—"

"You mean, has she gone to him? No. She's still at Cliveden House. Be damned if I can understand her these days. She avoids me, and when I do see her, she laughs and jabbers a lot of nonsense and then is flitting off with some fellow or—" Looking up, he saw the rigid expression and said, "For God's sake man, why put up with it? She's your wife! If you care for her—" Cliveden's flashing glare answered that. "Then fight for her! Grab her by the hair if need be, and drag the silly chit back here where she belongs."

"She said I cheated her into marriage," Cliveden muttered. "And she was right. It was a dishonourable business from start to finish."

"Fustian! I thought so at first, which was why I was so damnably irked with you. But I knew *why* you'd done it, which was why I kept still. Besides, you didn't warrant having a hole blown through you!"

"Helena had nothing to do with that! But d'you think I'm going to demand she stay with me when she loves another man? Would *you* want a woman, knowing your slightest touch revolted her? Thank you. No."

Hammond shrugged. "Well, there's not much time to change your mind, friend. Eastleigh has kept himself least in sight, but now he's off to Ceylon, I hear. Certainly, he'll never dare show his face in England again."

Whitening, Cliveden asked, "When?"

"Momentarily, I gather. He goes unmourned."

"And—does he also go alone?"

Hammond made his way to the window. "You know better than that."

"I see." So she was going with him, braving even exile for the man she loved. Cliveden drew a steadying breath, then said lightly, "Here comes Fulton at long last. You'll stay and take breakfast, I hope?"

Despite the casual tone, the line had been drawn and Hammond knew better than to attempt to continue his efforts. Sighing, he said, "I don't know who's the bigger fool. You—or my sister!"

"I CANNOT IMAGINE," grumbled Leopold Savage, guiding his curricle through London's stifling and busy streets, "why I am constantly caught up in such unsavoury kettles of soup. I vow, Nell, did I not adore you so passionately, I'd wash my hands of your entire clan!"

"You cannot," she said, smiling at him. "My brother is to wed your sister in three weeks' time, remember? You are fairly trapped, sir."

He looked at her fondly. She wore a pale lavender morning dress, with an inset yoke of white lace set off by little amethyst buttons. Her bonnet was of lavender straw lined with tiny ruffles of white lace and tied with white ribbons, and she carried a frilly lavender parasol to shield her delicate complexion from the hot summer sun. Her dark eyes smiled at him, her dainty little nose was beyond compare, her mouth almost too kissable to resist, and she was the most bewitching Fair he ever would see....

A carter shouted wrathfully, and horses squealed and reared. Very red in the face, Savage corrected his straying team and advised Helena that she should not be allowed out on the roads where she caused a poor fellow to lose what few wits she had left him. "I hope you know that you are allowing the chance of a life-time to pass you by," he went on, when they were clear of the imbroglio. "Let me point out in all modesty that I am dashing, charming, handsome, and rich. I can offer you a castle in Scotland, a cottage in the Shires, a nice house in Town, and a farm in Devonshire. Fur-thermore, if you don't accept me, I've every intention of putting a pistol to my head!"

"When?" she asked with interest.

He groaned. "Cruel one—I mean it!"

Her hand rested on his arm. She said gently, "I know you do, my dear. And I am so proud and happy to think you would want me to wife after—"

"Well, I do. And you'll have to marry someone, divine creature. You've thrown Cliveden over, and you don't want Eastleigh."

She said stonily, "Who will leave the country. Thank heaven!"

"Taking some misguided girl with him, no doubt," he appended, his face suddenly grim. "Gad, but it's a pity he shot before time, Nell! Cliveden could have rid the world of the cur!"

She said quietly, "Peter would not have shot to kill, at all events. He's an honourable man, Leo."

After a silent moment while he guided the team ever northward, he said with deep inner reluctance, "Sure you don't want to go back to him?"

She looked away quickly. "I cannot. He must know that Robert has now been disinherited. He would think I was crawling back to him only for—for his money. Besides," she stifled a sigh, "he can only despise me. When he caught me with Robert that dreadful night, and—"

"*Those* dreadful *nights*."

Startled, her eyes flew to his face.

He shrugged. "I was one of his seconds, remember? The night before the duel I came to collect him just after he'd seen you running across the flagway to your phaeton. He insisted we follow. He saw you leave Eastleigh's with whatever the gift was that he gave you. Cliveden didn't much like it, neither," he added, in a masterly piece of understatement.

"Dear...heaven!" moaned Helena, who had completely forgotten the little clock. "He must have thought—" She gave a stifled exclamation, then said pleadingly, "Robert had already left, Leo."

"Ain't none of my bread and butter, sweeting. If it had been, the *first* time I found you at Eastleigh's flat, I'd have called *him* out, as Cliveden did; and dragged *you* out, as he did; and spanked you all the way home—which I collect he did not."

"I fell asleep. Robert had given me some extreme potent wine."

"*What?* Why that filthy hound! Small wonder Cliveden wanted to blow his head off!" She looked distressed, so he took up her hand and kissed it. "What a naughty tippler! But naughty or not, I still want you, love."

His blue eyes were uncharacteristically earnest; he had been so loyal, so kind, and would probably make her a good and devoted husband. She held his hand tightly. "Give me a little time, Leo. I am very fond of you, and—"

Savage stood up in the curricle and let out a howl that so terrified the horses they bolted. Flung back onto the seat, he grappled the reins until a more decorous pace was achieved, then turned to Helena. "Sorry m'dear," he said jubilantly. "But that's the first time you've come close to accepting me! Jupiter! I'm dashed near bowled out!"

Helena smiled at him, but she was remembering how skilfully Peter had handled the team that afternoon in Tunbridge Wells, and wondering why she hadn't realized at the time how very happy she was....

For a space Savage was quiet and thoughtful. Then he said, "Look Nell, this is a long way and a silly waste of time. Why don't we turn back? I'll gather a Special License along the way, and we can be married this afternoon."

Amused, she answered, "I told you I must have a little time."

"I gave you a good three minutes," he said with an aggrieved air. "Ain't that enough? Very well—another three minutes, but no longer, mind!"

"A lot longer, you crazy creature! Ask me again next month." Ignoring his dismayed wail, she went on, "Where are we going, by the way? Doesn't the lady live in Town?"

"Lord no. Miles out in the country. And why you'd want to go and wish her happy, when it's your husband she's snared, I cannot comprehend."

"I know, I know. But—I just want to see what she's like. To make sure she will," her voice dropped "will be—good to him."

Savage looked at her sideways, and scowled, but said no more until they came to a wide heath where he warned her that troops of bloodthirsty highwaymen lurked, and they should turn back before they were set upon. Helena only laughed at him. When they reached sleepy Hampstead Village, he tried again to dissuade her, and failing, grumbled that he wished he'd never admitted that he knew where the wretched woman lived.

He pulled up the curricle before a charming and good-sized cottage set back in a well-kept garden. It was not at all the type of house Helena had expected, and she was more surprised when a neat maid answered Savage's knock and ushered them into a tastefully furnished parlour.

Waiting while her card was carried in, Helena whispered, "What is she like, Leo? Have you ever met her?"

"Saw her once, years ago. Perfectly ravishing. Rage of London. This is bound to be awful, Nell. A gentleman's wife don't call on his peculiar. For Lord's sake let's go and get the—"

"This way, if you please ma'am," said the maid.

Helena was led up a flight of winding stairs, along a short hall and into a—bedchamber! Her astonished gaze had scarcely time to take in the very cosy and feminine room before it became fixed upon the lady who lay in the four-poster. A delicate creature this, clad in a rich green satin bed jacket, her luxuriant hair confined by a lace-frilled cap. Great blue eyes searched Helena's face; a thin hand reached out, then was shyly withdrawn.

Stunned, Helena thought that Dorothy Grey had undoubtedly been a great beauty at one time, and there were still vestiges of beauty in the ravaged features, but only the eyes retained their original glory. The skin was puckered and drawn, and in places very smooth and shiny, pulling one side of the mouth down; her throat was cruelly scarred; pain had etched deep lines beside the small nose and between the brows; and the thick curls that must once have been a rich gold, were now almost white.

A hesitant voice said, "I am so very glad to meet you, Mrs. Cliveden. Pray forgive me for receiving you like this. I sometimes leave my room, and I would assuredly have been carried downstairs had I known you were to call. Peter has told me so much about you. I—I hope you do not—hate me."

This was the lady he meant to marry? Why the pitiful little thing must be more than a decade older than he, and looked to be a complete invalid! Recovering her wits with an effort, Helena put out her hand and advanced with her warmest smile. Miss Grey's fingers were so fragile she scarcely dared to press them, and they trembled in hers, while the great blue eyes regarded her with distinct trepidation.

"Of course I am not outraged," she said gently. And pulling up the chair that was eagerly indicated,

she went on, "I came because—because I thought you
might be—worrying."

The twisted but bravely rouged lower lip trembled.
Blinking, Miss Grey said, "How very kind. I have
been frantic. Peter is always so good about coming to
see me, I knew something must be wrong. And when
I heard he had been shot down by that unspeakable
craven...!" Her eyes flashed fire for a moment, then
she asked, "How does your husband go on, ma'am?
I pray he is improved? I heard he was—" her voice
faltered "—at death's door."

Helena patted the frail hand and released it. "He
had a very narrow escape, and is still not completely
recovered, which is why he has not visited you. But—
he asked that I thank you so much for the beautiful
violets."

"Ah! So you knew they were from me. I was so
troubled about sending them, for I know how the dear
man worships you, and not for the world would I—
Heavens! I have upset you!"

Helena fumbled for her handkerchief. "Forgive
me," she said with a shaken little laugh. "But—I have
been under a great shadow."

Miss Grey leaned forward, peering at the expres-
sive face of this beauteous young bride. "Poor child.
Peter is one in a thousand, but— He *did* tell you
about—us?" Her eyes narrowed as Helena's fell, and
seeing the faint blush, the helpless gesture, she went
on, "Why that rascal! And you came here expecting...what, I wonder? A buxom bird of paradise,
perhaps?"

Helena ventured an upward glance and met a twin-
kling look. Her hand went out again and was warmly
clasped and they laughed together.

"Yet you came at all events," said Miss Grey, lying
back and shaking her head incredulously. "Ah, but
my Peter has found a lady who deserves him! No—not
a word, Mrs. Cliveden, until I have told you what
happened...."

"DO YOU KNOW WHAT I THINK, Leo," said Helena,
her eyes brighter than he had ever seen them. "I think
you knew all about it, and that is why you did not
want me to come. You knew she was Peter's—*inamorata* when he was in college and she was, as you put
it, the 'Rage of London.' And I think you knew that
the theatre caught fire and she was so terribly burned,
and left to die when she could no longer afford to pay
the doctor." Savage guided his team through the
darkening streets and grunted sourly, but Helena's
eyes softened. She murmured tenderly, "How typical
of him. Everyone else deserted her, and she was ill and
without funds, her health and her looks gone, poor
little soul. But Peter heard about it, and found her,
and all these years he's seen to it that she never went
hungry or was neglected. He bought her that little
house, and made her a regular allowance, and—"

"And now you know that he's no intention of mar-
rying her. Especially since he's only eight and twenty,
and she's—"

"Leo! For shame! And if you knew, wicked one,
why did you not tell me?"

He said quietly, "I have played my hand poorly enough by taking you to see her, so that you could be—very sure of your heart." Helena squeezed his hand with silent gratitude. He looked away, then went on in his usual tones, "I thought you'd never come out! Here it is half past seven already, and a fine storm blowing up unless I mistake it. We'll be lucky do we reach my house before dark, and I give you warning Nell, I mean to change teams and have something to eat before I take you home! If ever I knew two women to talk for less than..."

He grumbled on, but Helena scarcely heard him. In a few short hours her grey and desolate world had become a sunlit paradise; her formerly heavy heart now sang with happiness, and yet by a strange paradox she could have wept, her emotions were so intense. She had known for some time that she loved the husband she had driven away. For a longer time, she had realized that he was a brave gentleman with a high sense of honour. Not until today, however, had she truly known how deeply she was loved; not until the poor little broken lady in the cottage had told her story had she realized that Peter loved deeply enough to make the ultimate sacrifice—to give her up and clear the way for her to marry the man he loathed, but whom he thought she idolized. He'd said he was to marry his *inamorata* only so that she would feel less guilty about leaving him. 'Oh, Peter,' she thought yearningly, 'I'll come to you, my own. I'll make you as happy as is within my power, my dear, generous, gallant love.'

It was raining steadily when they approached Sackville Street. Savage cursed under his breath, and turned the horses into the rear alley where were his stables.

Trying to shield them both with her parasol, Helena thought, 'Poor Leo,' and peeping at him repentantly, was surprised to see his expression grim and murderous.

"Well if that don't put the wolf in with the porkers," he snarled, and pulled back on the reins.

Why on earth would he stop here, when they were almost to—Helena's bewilderment was cut off by fright. Three men, wearing dark riding coats, low-drawn hats, and their faces hideously masked, blocked the way. A short distance beyond, a closed carriage was barely visible in the rainy dusk. She shrank against Savage. "Don't stop! Charge them!"

"Cannot charge three horse pistols with you beside me," he said angrily. "A fine mess you've got me into, Nell!"

"But, if we—"

"You—Lord Wet and Whiney," snarled the tallest of the three, who was evidently the leader. "Out!"

Savage said furiously, "You'll swing on Tyburn Tree for this, rogue!"

"You can get out or be blowed out." The heavyset individual to the right of the leader, drew back the hammer of his pistol.

Cursing under his breath, Savage jumped down and turned to help Helena.

The third man rode forward, coming so close to Savage that he was forced to step back or be trampled. "Damn you," he raged. "What the devil— Hey!"

Helena had been watching Savage so anxiously that she'd not noticed the other two ruffians walk their horses to her side of the curricle. Without warning, the tall man leaned down. She shrieked as his arms swept around her. Kicking, fighting, she was dragged from the curricle. A hand was clamped over her mouth. She beat her parasol at her captor's head until his accomplice wrenched the parasol away and growled, "You want us to slit yer friend's throat, missus? Keep wriggling!" These were desperate men, perhaps starving men, who probably would not balk at murder. She must not be responsible for dear Leo being hurt. Helpless, she stopped struggling.

The leader turned his horse and rode to the carriage; the second man opened the door, and Helena was lowered into his arms while the leader dismounted and swung inside. Tossed in after him, she threw out her hands instinctively, and they were caught and held strongly. Comprehension came like a heavy blow. Robert! Of course!

"No!" she gasped frantic and furious. "I won't go with you!"

His answer was to slam the door. With one arm he grabbed her with such ruthless strength that she could scarcely move; and his other hand again clamped over her mouth. The carriage began to jolt over the cobblestones. Fighting back tears of despair, Helena thought in anguish that she had been so close—so very close to happiness at last.

After a few minutes he let her go, and her dazed mind began to try and reason. To struggle was pointless; he was too strong for her, and if she fought, he'd

probably have her tied, which would be horrid. Leo
had said Robert meant to take a woman out of the
country with him; she should have guessed she would
be his victim. Her bones were melting with fear, but
she said with all the contempt she could convey, "You
must know what I think of you." When he did not
answer, she went on bravely, "Nothing you could do
would *ever* make me love you."

"No...?" His laugh was low-pitched and she
thought it the most sinister sound she'd heard in all her
life.

She bit her lip hard to keep from weeping, and demanded, "How could you want a lady who despises
you and loves another man? I cannot bring you happiness."

"And I cannot be happy without you. Helena," he
pulled her close, his voice hoarse with emotion, "I
can't let you go!"

She struggled wildly. "Don't touch me! You are
loathsome, and—"

But he did touch her. She was dragged even closer;
his hand grabbed the back of her hair and jerked her
head back. His lips found hers and she was kissed despite her frantic efforts to be free—kissed with a passion, a hunger that awoke a soaring excitement, and
set her heart to beating crazily. Dimly, she despised
herself, but the emotion was swept away by the ec-
stasy of that long embrace. When it ended, she was
weak and gasping for breath. Robert had never kissed
her like that. Only once in her life had she known such
dear delight... And that had been when—She stiffened.

"Peter Cliveden!" she exclaimed, tearing off his mask.

"Very true," he admitted. "I had to guard against others recognizing me, else I'd not have resorted to such tactics."

Her heart gave a great leap of exhilaration. "You are abducting me!"

"So it would seem."

Aching with love for him, she could not refrain from punishing him a little for frightening her so, and said sternly, "Then your promise to grant me a divorce was another lie, sir?"

"I must have been out of my mind to ever make such a promise. You should have run to him while I was still too ill to think clearly. Why did you not?"

"I—ah, was waiting for your solicitor to bring the legal documents," she said, smiling happily into the darkness. "You *did* make some arrangements?"

Choosing to ignore this home thrust, he said, "I gave you up because you'd been so kind as to stay with me when I was ill and you might so easily have slipped away. But I knew with each day that passed what a sorry fool I'd been. You may loathe and despise me, ma'am, but be damned if I'll let you go to a rogue who would only drag you down to degradation. I think I might have stood it had you chosen Savage. But— Eastleigh! No, by God!"

Rejoicing, Helena sighed, "Poor Leo. And he had just proposed again."

"Had he! Then he has my sympathy. He'll not be harmed, never fear. But he'll never call you wife, I promise you."

"I see. The male animal. All brute beast, complete with horrid oaths and bruising hands. And I had thought you so gentle...Mr. Cliveden."

She felt him tense. He said uncertainly, "You had?"

"And kind. Even to the cats." Her lips quirked as she heard his sudden intake of breath. "You hurt my poor—"

"Poor—what?"

"Wrist. Just here..." She held it up for inspection, and it was at once kissed.

Trying not to shiver, she said, "And here..." And after a blissful moment, "And...worst of all... here..."

"Helena...?" His voice shook. "Oh, my Helena... Do you mean—Can you mean...?"

She tapped the afflicted area with a demanding finger.

Cliveden gasped again, then bent and attended to the hurt. Thoroughly.

When they were both more or less recovered, Helena lay contentedly in his arms. By the light of the flambeaux outside a house they passed he saw the tenderness in her smile, and his pulses leapt. "Helena," he murmured. "Did you not mind being abducted?"

"I did indeed mind! It was horrid! Especially since...I thought it was—Robert."

"Oh...God!" Awed by this miracle, he stammered, "Do you say you—you didn't *want* to go with him?"

"I wanted to be with my husband, only—" She put up both hands and held him back firmly, but very carefully. "Only," she went on demurely, "since he is getting married again soon, I knew I must keep away."

"Oh! My Lord! Helena! There is something—I mean—I must tell you—"

"Where are you taking me, my cruel abductor?"

"To Whisperwood, of course. But, Helena—I wasn't quite—"

"You seem much better, sir. Very strong, in fact."

"Yes. I am quite recovered, thanks to you. But I must tell you that Dorothy Grey is—"

"A very dear and kind lady," she finished, smiling up at him.

"What?"

"I went to see her this morning. You lied to and deceived me again, didn't you, Mr. Cliveden?"

He took one of her little hands and began to kiss each finger. "I fear I did, madam wife."

"If I were to ask you a question," she said, holding up the thumb he had overlooked, "just for once, could you give me an honest answer?"

"Most cherished of all women," he said, when he had finished with the thumb, "I will try my best."

"I was wondering," she said shyly, "is your... bedchamber finished yet... my most gallant husband?"

He lifted her to his lips, loving her, worshipping her, hardly able to believe that so much happiness had come his way. And—when he had the breath—he answered huskily, "Ready and waiting—my most beautiful beloved."

"In that case," she said matter-of-factly, "I think, if we were to have warming pans put between the sheets, we might—"

"I promise you," he interrupted, "that we will have no need of warming pans...."

"Indeed?" she said, her eyes wide and guileless. "Why ever not?"

His lips twitched. "Why, because the—er, the cats will keep the sheets warm of course... my Helena."

"How nice for us... my darling, *darling* Peter...."

They said few words after that, but some hours later Helena discovered that once again her husband had—to an extent—deceived her. Actually, the cats had nothing to do with keeping them warm that night.